THE CONCRETE JUNGLE

Written By

Rico Garcia

CONCRETE JUNGLE(2019)
An Urban Melodrama

WRITTEN BY : Rico Garcia

Synopsis

ACT1

David is our hero exemplified by his humble demeanor, It's present day in Denver Colorado on "Tha Eastside". A once predominantly black neighborhood flourished with black business and entertainment has transitioned from housing projects and the crack epidemic now to Denver's Newest urban development project. Billy, once one of David's best friends is a King Pin unaware his connect T.C. short for "Too Cool" is a government informant.

David is haunted by the murder of his best friend Kareem and often drifts into flashbacks from the early 1990's. David was wild, Kareem was his sidekick and Billy was the kid everyone picked on. Ironically it was T.C. Who helped change that, influencing Billy to kill his mom abuser as a 10year old child. David's and Billy's fathers were murdered together and were also active Crip gang members. Billy's mom smoked crack, David's mom abandoned him as an infant, growing up Billy and David made an inseparable bond until 3years after Kareem's death his Father Shahid was also murdered, and by crips.

David is always on the move working to accomplish his goal of "Buying back the block!". One day he's in the bank applying for a loan and runs into a girl from his childhood named Queen. Queen is now a military woman as beautiful as could be, she's in town helping with her sick Grandmother. While David rekindles the flame with Queen another Woman from his past becomes obsessively jealous. Delilah, sexy, glamorous and ratchet grew up with David, Billy, Kareem and Queen. When Billy started hustling, Delilah started behind him. Billy and David haven't spoke since Shahid's assassination. Delilah and Billy speak everyday, along with moving weight Delilah is a renegade prostitute. When Delilah gets her opportunity to make a move on David she does, and this is where things get messy. Delilah is married to Jason Johnson former NBA prospect turned stay at home loser that spies on her every move through the iPad he has synced with her iPhone.

FADE IN:

EXT. 5 POINTS - MIDDAY

A small gathering of people crowds around apartment grand opening, Billy is seen getting out of his car casually dressed in blue, a white woman can be heard speaking into a mega phone.

INTERCUT TOURISTS ATTRACTIONS, SKIING AS NARRATION BEGINS

                    DAVID(O.S.)
This is my home, Denver Colorado. I'm sure you probably heard of it, the first place to legalize recreational usage of marijuana. Or maybe you're a fan of the XGAMES or skiing. You may have flown into DIA and visited some of the many tourists' attractions available year-round. If you been to Denver recently you've probably been stuck in traffic due to the high volume of people moving in from out of town, you probably also noticed new development everywhere. Like all these new apartments and businesses being built on the E, now referred to by the white media as Rhino. But whenever something bad happens here they'll refer to this community as it's rightful name the 5points. It's funny how that is, it's been a pattern between unsolved murders, to people who left with no evidence of ever having existed. And now the city is attempting to erase a whole community, a culture of people that gave life to this place before you knew life even existed here.

                                        CUT TO:

EXT. 5 POINTS MIDDAY

Front facing focused directly on David

                    DAVID (CONTINUES.)
That's me, I'm trying to keep it cool, but I'm pissed off!

                                        CUT TO:

Front facing soft focus directly on Billy

DAVID (CONTINUES.)
And behind me that's Billy, I'm not sure if he's bothered by any of this at all.

DISSOLVE TO:

Billy with homies surrounding him on looking the demonstration

CRIP1
Cuz turn this shit down right quick, y'all see this shit nigga? This that re-generation bullshit they doing right here in the hood cuz.

CRIP2
CUZ SHUT UP FOO, ITS CALLED GENTRIFICATION.

CRIP1
You know what the fuck I meant.

CRIP2
And that shit ain shit anyways so... we moving on up, out the hood. Shit somebody gotta move in it.

CRIP1
Naw it's a trick to this shit, remember this shit was fucked up when we had it, they could've did all this new shit then... Billy know what the fuck I'm talking about.

BILLY

Man I don't give a fuck about none of that bullshit, every last one of them crazy honkeys gonna be snorting coke and they all gonna be getting it from me watch!

Close up crawl zoom to Billy's face

      DAVID (O.S.)
Man Billy has changed a lot, I remember a time when he was so different, we all were so different, everything was so different.

      BILLY
This gentrification shit gone make us rich cuz, on the game.

         FADE TO BLACK

Title screen

         FADE UP:

EXT. OUTSIDE ELEMENTARY SCHOOL - AFTERNOON

Close up crawl zoom out from 10-year-old Billy's face, other kids surround a distraught Billy laughing as they make fun of him.

      KID1
Like I was saying, you dirty, you poor, and you stink! (kids burst into laughter) you smell like hot dog water and dirty clothes (Kids laugh louder)

         CUT TO:

INT. PRINCIPALS OFFICE - END OF SCHOOL DAY

Elegantly dressed older Black Woman accompanied by her driver stand talking with principal as David and Kareem walk in.

                    PRINCIPAL
                 Here's David now

                   MS. COUSINS
                   Which one?

David steps forward

                      DAVID
            That's me, what's cracking

                    PRINCIPAL
       Language Mr. Williams, Kareem do you have to
              go everywhere David goes?

                     KAREEM
         Of course, I do (boys start laughing)

Ms. Cousins glares down at David

                   MS. COUSINS
                    Look up.

David gives Ms. Cousins a quizzical look

                      DAVID
                      What?

                   MS. COUSINS
          Hmm. (Nostrils flare with disdain)

Ms. Cousins directs her attention back to Principal

                   MS. COUSINS

                    Thanks, dear.

Ms Cousins pats principal on the back before exiting room with driver trailing behind her.

                                        DISSOLVE TO:

EXT. OUTSIDE OF SCHOOL - END OF SCHOOL DAY

INTERCUT KIDS MAKING FUN OF BILLY, DELILAH WALKING WITH QUEEN

                    KID2
     Look at this niggas shoes! (Kids Burst out
                  laughing)

David and Kareem come walking up

                    DAVID
     Why don't you shut the fuck up alright?

The circle of a crowd breaks as David and Kareem walk thru

Queen has a picture she drew for David that she is now showing Delilah

                    QUEEN
     Delilah look at what I made for David today

David stands toe to toe with Kid2

                    DAVID
     You a mark Calvin, just like yo punk ass
                    Daddy.

                    KAREEM
     Sure, you're right! (Kids start laughing)

You can see that Delilah is jealous of the drawing

> DELILAH
> Oh, it's alright, isn't LowDown his gang banger name?

> QUEEN
> Yeah?

> DELILAH
> I thought you didn't like gangs?

Walking amongst the crowd of kids locking C's with Billy before eventually finding platform above the crowd

> DAVID
> This is crip cuz! I don't give a fuck about what none of y'all got going on. You hear me? This crip!

> KAREEM
> Crip gang, crip, crip, crip gang!

Queen holding out picture smiling and admiring her work

> QUEEN
> I know, but ain it cute?! I know he'll like it.

Kid1 steps towards Kareem

> KID1
> Kareem my dad was talking to your dad the other night, and your dad said you're a wanna be crip (Crowd laughs)

Delilah rolling her eyes with contempt for queen and her drawing

> DELILAH
> Whatever, and you know I liked David first so why would you even try that?

> QUEEN
> What??

Queen stops in her tracks

David jumps down in front of kid1

> DAVID
> Wannabe this (CLAP!)

David punches kid1 in the face, Kareem jumps in to help David as they both beat up kid1, Queen and Delilah come and break up the fight.

> DELILAH
> David are you okay?

> DAVID
> Yea I'm good, just some marks

Delilah snatches picture out of Queens back pocket

> DELILAH
> Look what queen made for you, it was my idea

Queen snatches picture back

> QUEEN
> This was not! Your idea.

David Snatches picture from Queen

                    DAVID
    I don't care whose idea it was, this shit is
        cracking cuz! Kareem, Billy, look at this
                shit. LOWDOWN! On the game!

A car pulls up and starts honking.

                    QUEEN
        Okay D, there go yo daddy (Queen snickering)

                    DELILAH
        That is not my dad, that is my driver

Delilah heads to get in car

                    QUEEN
                Bye girl!

                                    FADE TO:

EXT. FIVE POINTS NEIGHBORHOOD - LATE AFTERNOON

David Billy Kareem And Queen walk each other home from school, they arrive at queens house the first stop.

                    DAVID
            Alright Queen, here's your stop

                    QUEEN
        Thanks for always walking me home David.

Kareem making fun of David, Billy laughs a little

                    DAVID

Of course, and I know it wasn't Delilah's idea to make me this. I don't know what's up with that girl.

                QUEEN
Yea, but you think she's, pretty don't you.

                DAVID
(Un assuredly) What?

                QUEEN
Wow, you like her too huh?

                DAVID
Hold up, I ain saying all that

                QUEEN
You don't have to. You like her, you think she's pretty and you'd pick her over me

Queen pushes by David heading to her door

                DAVID
Queen you're my best friend

Queen does not turn around, she continues to storm off as she exits the scene

                QUEEN
Whatever David, enjoy your summer. and your stupid ass picture

                DAVID
Queen!

Door slams, Kareem and Billy laugh

                KAREEM

C'mon playa! I thought you replace em not chase em

DAVID
(Laughing) shut up foo

FADE TO:

Billy Kareem and David now arrive in front of Billy's house

DAVID
Alright Billy

The three boys shake each other's hands

BILLY
Thanks for sticking up for me, it's just-

DAVID
Look save all that, I understand besides our pops died together, you always crip in my eyes

Billy's eyes light up, smiles from ear to ear

BILLY
Alright guys, later, (Takes of running to house) have a good summer

DISSOLVE TO:

David and Kareem arrive home in front of Kareem's house, the two are excited shadow boxing highlights from their fight earlier.

KAREEM
I had to hit em with the left!

DAVID

That left was cold too, I was like woah ok cuz
(Both laugh)

              KAREEM
Man, it's gonna be a wild summer. I'm at city park every Sunday, every Sunday.

              DAVID
On me cuz (more laughter)

Kareem opening front door with key

              KAREEM
You know my pops gone hate tho

              DAVID
Shiiit

David stops at door without going in

              KAREEM
What you doing?

              DAVID
I ain going in there.

              KAREEM
Cuz, you know my pops be tripping if we don't come home first

              DAVID
I know, it's summertime. I'm staying out here, you know where to find me.

The boys lock C's

              KAREEM
You lucky

David walking away smiling

                    DAVID
     Remember what yo pops said, it's never luck.
               It's God! (Laughs)

                    KAREEM
                 Alright cuz!

                                        FADE TO:

INT. DELILAH'S HOUSE - EARLY EVENING

Delilah's watching T.V. While her dad cooks in the kitchen when Delilah's mom comes thru the front door.

                    MOM
                 I'm home!

                    DAD
             Hey boo, I missed you

Delilah's dad goes in to kiss her mom while she's taking her shoe's off, she blocks him when he gets near.

                    MOM
         Uh-uh you smell like raw meat

                    DAD
                I was cooking

                    MOM
            (Sarcastically) Really?

Mom turns her face towards Delilah and rolls her eyes

                    MOM

                    What did you make?

                          DAD
                (Reluctantly) Fish tacos.

Mom Now walking towards Delilah

                          MOM
        Okay, gone with ya bad self, Delilah what you
                         doing?

                        DELILAH
                      Watching T.V.

                          MOM
          I see that, now get your feet off my
        mothafucking table. What's wrong with you
                      little girl?

                        DELILAH
                        Nothing.

                          MOM
              Come here and give me some sugar

Delilah gets up and her mom kisses both her cheeks and gives her a hug. Dad goes back to kitchen

                          MOM
          I'll be right back I'm bout to get out these
                    clothes and shower.

Delilah nods her head, she looks disappointed and goes to sit back down, her mom goes upstairs. Then Delilah gets up to say something to her dad.

                        DELILAH

                          Dad. I thought you were going to check her?

                                    DAD
                                 Check her?

                                  DELILAH
                   Yes, you were talking to Grandma about how
                          you're tired of this shit.

Delilah's Dad cover her mouth

                                    DAD
                      SHH! You weren't supposed to hear that.

Delilah throws dads hands away

                                  DELILAH
                   Get your hands off of me! They smell like raw
                                    meat.
Delilah walks away mumbling

                                  DELILAH
                              You are so weak.

                                                              CUT TO:

INT. BILLY'S LIVING ROOM - EARLY EVENING

Billy sits on the floor making a house of
cards on a coffee table, his mom Laverne comes
out of a back room.

                                  LAVERNE
                        Billy, I need you to go outside.

                                   BILLY
                          I don't wanna go outside.

                                  LAVERNE

Not with this bullshit right now.I said go outside boy.

                BILLY
(Mousy voice) But I'm just playing right here.

SLAP! Billy's mom slaps Billy across the face.

              LAVERNE
Mothafucka I said go outside

Billys mom repeatedly strikes him, Billy curls into a ball black himself yelling

              BILLY
I want my mom back! I want my mom back!

              LAVERNE
I am your mom motha-

Door flys open, Ray the local Crack Dealer walks in with his friend Travis

              RAY
What the fuck is all this?

Ray slowly makes his way to the couch, Travis slide in and closes the door

              LAVERNE
I was just telling him to go outside. How you doing Ray?

              RAY
What? This my nigga Travis
              LAVERNE
              Hi.

Travis nods what's up

                    RAY
    Lil nigga shut up all that crying and go
              outside. Come here.

Billy gets up and stands in front of Ray. Ray
mushes his face and lightly smacks the back of
Billy's head.

                    RAY
  Peanut head ass boy, I still can't believe you
  really yo daddy son. Look go outside and play
                 lil nigga.

                                        CUT TO:

EXT. BILLYS FRONT PORCH - EARLY EVENING

Door slams behind billy on front porch, David
is walking by with 2 other kids dressed in
blue.

                    DAVID
   Billy what's cracking cuz what you doing
  outside? You ain smoking them rocks with yo
                mom today?!

Billy is moping and sits on his porch

                    BILLY
              I don't know

                    DAVID
  Look my bad cuz damn, it's just a joke… man
  cuz you need to get off that sad shit all the
  time cuz… we'll we headed to Curtis park if
             you wanna come foo.

                    BILLY

It's ok David go without me.

                      DAVID
                Suit yourself..

Billy sits on porch time passes Ray and Travis leave, Billy goes inside to see mom in her room beat up.

                                      FADE TO:

INT. LAVERNES ROOM -EVENING

Billy's eyes double in size, he runs over to his mom who is on the floor, she stops him in his tracks and pushes him away.

                      BILLY
Momma! What happened?! What happened momma?
                    LAVERNE
Boy c'mon with all that screaming before I black your eye too.

                    BILLY
              What happened?

                  LAVERNE
What you think? Look boy I need you to go to the creamery and get me some ice and a burrito.

                    BILLY
        Can I have one too?

                  LAVERNE
    Boy don't play with me..

                                      FADE TO:

EXT. IN FRONT OF CREAMERY - EVENING

Billy walks dragging his shoulders face to the ground.

SHOCCA (O.S.)
CA-RRRIP! Billy!! What up boy!?

Shocca is smiling from ear to ear, with his arms in an expression to say what's up, he has on a gold chain and blue kangol hat, he is also accompanied by T.C.. Billy runs to Shocca gives him a handshake and hug.

BILLY
Shocca!

SHOCCA
What's up lil cuz?

BILLY
I thought they said you was never getting out? You know for what happened to those cops.

SHOCCA
(Laughing) I probably wasn't, if it wasn't for the homie T.C.. He use to run with yo pops and Big Low Down back in the gap.

T.C is full of gold from rings to frames and teeth. He flicks a cigarette butt.

T.C.
Who's this?

SHOCCA
This Billy, Shocca son.

T.C.

                    Oh okay, what's up lil man

T.C attempts to lock C's with Billy, Billy
pulls his hand away

                         SHOCCA
                      He don't bang.

T.C has his eyes locked on Billy, calculating

                          T.C.
                      And why not?

                         SHOCCA
              Ay Billy how's your mom doing?

Billy shakes his head and stares at the floor
looking sad.

                         SHOCCA
        What's wrong? C'mon little homie what I tell
         you about all this weird ass shit, what's
                   wrong with yo momma?

                         BILLY
         Ray and his friend came and beat her up and
                          stuff.

                         SHOCCA
                      Damn Laverne..

Shocca wraps his arm around Billy

                          T.C.
        Is that your moms boyfriend or something?

                         SHOCCA
                   Ay T.C. I got this.

                          T.C.
        Hold up, this nigga beating on your mom, that
          shits dead today. Big Shocca was yo pops
                          right?

                         SHOCCA
                       T.C. Cuz-

                          T.C.
         What nigga? Billy, Big Shocca was yo pops
                          right?

Billy nods his head yes.

                          T.C.
       Well I owe yo pops, for everything I have. So
       I'm a handle these niggas for you okay? Okay?

                         BILLY
                           OK

                          T.C.
                But your coming with me.

                                             FADE TO:

INT. ABANDONED BUILDING - NIGHT

Ray is beat up sprawling across floor bleeding
from his mouth and face, Shocca and T.C. Are
sweaty from beating up ray, T.C removes his
gloves and pulls out pistol in front of a
shocked Billy. Shocca is exhausted striking
Ray one last time.

                          T.C.
         (Out of breathe) That's good cuz. Come here
       Billy, is this the lil bitch that beat up your

mom? Yea? On the way here you said he raped her a couple times too. You hear that Ray? Look at him Billy all crying and scared and shit now. You know why? Cause this is crip!

T.C. Pistol whips Ray

              T.C. (CONT'D)
It's time for you to come home Billy, you Big Shocca son! I want you to do this for your mom Billy, but really you doing it for your dad.-

              SHOCCA
           T.C. Man.

              T.C.
Most importantly tho you doing this for crip, look.

T.C. crouches down Grabs Billy's hand and places it around the gun.

            T.C.(CONT'D)
   How that gun feel in your hand?

             SHOCCA
           Ay Cuz!

            T.C.(CONT'D)
   It's alright you can smile.

              SHOCCA
T.C what the fuck is you doing my nigga?!

T.C. Rises up abruptly to confront Shocca
              T.C.
Shocca, I really need you to get on the same page my nigga, You with me or against me?

                         SHOCCA
                I'm with you my nigga bu-

                          T.C
        We'll be with me, I'm looking out for MY dead
         homies son. And you mothafucka stop moving!
                       Billy..(more)

T.C. Walks over to Billy crouches places gun
back in hand. Shocca leaves room.

                       T.C.(CONT'D)
     Now look here, you see that white dot? Aim it
          right in the middle of Rays head..(more)

Ray starts begging Billy for his life, he
continues.

                      T.C. (CONT'D)
       Ignore that, focus on me. Now line those two
         other white dot with the middle one. When
          you're ready to shoot just squeeze the
       trigger. Don't get scared now, you a natural.
       C'mon lil nigga, this piece of shit raped your
       mom right? Beats her right? This nigga try to
       act like he yo daddy! He makes your mom smoke
                crack and he bosses you around.

Billy locks in on ray who is still begging but
billy can't hear him, all he can hear is T.C.
And he's actually getting mad.

                     T.C. (CONT'D O/S)
         This nigga ain you daddy! Blow him away!
       Billy! All you gotta do is squeeze! What you
        think you're dad woulda done? Your dad loved
       your mom, do it for him. That's right Billy do
                    it for ya pops! Squeeze!

Close Big Gun BLAST!

                                          FADE TO:

Black Screen 25 years later..

                                          FADE TO:

INT. WELTON ST. CAFÉ – MIDDAY

Close on Billy's eyes, Billy is eating at Welton St. Café, the waitress walks buy and Billy orders a lemonade, Billy is wearing a few nice pieces with diamonds and designer clothing

                        BILLY
Let me get another lemonade, please

                    WAITRESS
Okay Billy, I'll go get that for you right now.

As the waitress goes to get Billy's drink T.C. walks in, he is much older now, and much more successful, everything brand new including his Rolex and gold wired frames, he addresses a few people with a simple head nod on his way in going straight to Billy's table

                        T.C.
Billy, what's the word

T.C. Has a seat in the only other empty chair at Billy's table

                        BILLY
Business as usual, getting to the money.

T.C.
Already, that's what I like to hear

Waitress returns with pink lemonade

WAITRESS
Excuse me. Okay, would you like to order anything?

T.C.
You got some yac back there?

WAITRESS
You know we don't have no yac

T.C.
(Chuckles) You know I'm playing. Let me get a ten extra crispy, honey hot.

WAITRESS
Alright, and Billy we're still working on your food okay?

BILLY
Alright

Waitress walks off

BILLY
So what's up with this meeting?

T.C.
Some friends of mine noticed a little bit of a problem we have right here in the neighborhood. We, well, they need to get into this neighborhood, but we got some people not quite willing to move-

BILLY
So what's the fuck that got to do with me?

                              T.C.
Listen. This has everything to do with you, it
      has a good outcome for both of us.

Billy squints and shoots a suspicious look at
T.C.

                              T.C.
Don't tell me you on this hold on to the
   Eastside shit? Look shit happening with or
without us, we gotta get in where we fit in my
nigga, all these years I've never steered you
                             wrong.

                             BILLY
              Naw it's nothing like that

                              T.C.
                    Well what's it like?

                             BILLY
Nothing, just tell me what you need me to do

                              T.C.
              We can start with ya David.

                                              CUT TO:

INT. BANK - MIDDAY

David stands impatiently in line to be seen at
the bank. He then taps the woman in front of
him on her shoulder.

                             DAVID
                          Excuse me?

Short petite Darker skinned black woman turns around and does a double take when she sees David.

> QUEEN
> Um..(pause) David??

David gives Queen a strong suspicious look before responding

> DAVID
> Queen?!? Wow!

David goes in for a hug and is stopped by the palm of Queens hand.

> QUEEN
> Hey, nice to see you again too(laughs)

> DAVID
> My bad, it's been forever last time I seen you hand to been, you was in 10th grade at George.

> QUEEN
> Yea..

Queen shoots David a suspicious look

> QUEEN
> I didn't see you there?

> DAVID
> Yea I stopped going to school after Kareem got popped freshmen year. I was a East Angel anyways tho.

> QUEEN
> Oh man, I rem hearing about that.

                    DAVID
    Yeah, so anyways are you just visiting? Where
                have you been?

                    QUEEN
    Gone, and when I'm done burying my grandma
              I'll be gone again.

                    DAVID
    I'm sorry to hear that she was really a nice
                   woman.

                    QUEEN
                 Thank you.

                    DAVID
    You know while you're in town it be nice to
          catch up. Have some coffee.

                    QUEEN
                  Coffee?

                    DAVID
    Yea, and actually I gotta go right now. Here's
              my business card,

David pull out business card and shows Queen

                 DAVID(CONTINUES)
    my cells on the bottom. It be nice to talk
          with you before you leave town.

David hands Queen his card and Exits.

                                        CUTS TO:

EXT. IN FRONT OF BANK ON WELTON ST. - MIDDAY

David scans the area, he spots a beautiful Mercedes Benz, driving is a beautiful light complected woman with long hair.

CUT TO:

INT. - MERCEDES BENZ - MIDDAY

Delilah notices David walk outside the bank as she speeds down the street playing loud music

                    DELILAH
  Well look at this, there go David fine broke ass.

Delilah honks horn as she drives by David, David waves in response.

CUT TO:

EXT. IN FRONT OF BANK ON WELTON ST. - MIDDAY

                    DAVID
        Hi Delilah, bye Delilah..

DISSOLVE TO:

INT. WELTON ST. CAFÉ - MIDDAY

Delilah walks in Welton st. Café looking glamorous, expensive, ratchet and beautiful.

                    DELILAH
                Hey girl!

                    WAITRESS
              Hey Delilah

                    DELILAH
Girl let me get the usual, I'm in a rush too.

                    WAITRESS
6 piece Honey Hot, Fries bread and strawberry
lemonade in a to go cup. And your in a rush.
                    DELILAH
                  Thanks boo

                    WAITRESS
                 Mmhm, $11.75

Delilah reaches into her handbag, when she
does this she also notices T.C. Sitting in the
restaurant with Billy.

                    DELILAH
   Is that T.C. over there? I'm a go say hi.

Delilah pays for her food and heads in T.C.
Direction.

                                        CUT TO:

INT.INSIDE WELTON ST. CAFE - MIDDAY

T.C. And Billy wrap up a conversation as
Delilah walks up.

                     T.C.
   I understand and I know you will too. Look
   Billy where doing something whether you like
                  it or not..

                    DELILAH
                   Hey T.C.

T.C. Looks to see that it's Delilah and gets
up from table

                         T.C.
                       Excuse me.

Delilah is left with a confused look on her
face, Billy is dying to laugh, He waits for
T.C. To walk away

                         BILLY
                Hmph.. (Bust our laughing)

                        DELILAH
              Whatever nigga, what's up Billy?

                         BILLY
                      Chilling Cuz.

                        DELILAH
         I just seen yo homeboy walking out the bank

                         BILLY
                          Who??

                        DELILAH
                     David.(giggles)
                         BILLY
            Ha, that's supposed to be funny huh

                        DELILAH
                 Ways out ways out(laughs)

                         BILLY
        He probably in there getting denied for a loan
                      or something

                        DELILAH
              Uh uh(laughs) you ain right..

                         BILLY

Naw, fr tho

DELILAH
Anyways, you got that

BILLY
You got that??

Billy rubs thumb and index finger together gesturing money.

DELILAH
Don't play me.

BILLY
Damn cuz, look at that bracelet!

Billy grabs Delilah's wrist to get a closer view before she pulls away.

BILLY (CONTINUES)
I'm saying tho, how you doing this, and everything else with what I'm giving you? Let me find out you out here renegading?

DELILAH
Wow, that's disrespectful..

BILLY
(Chuckles) How?

DELILAH
You just tried to call me a hoe on the low.

BILLY
And, if you was ain't nothing wrong with it, if you not then you just not.

DELILAH

                    Whatever nigga, you got my shit or what?

                              BILLY
                    Damn renega-, I mean Delilah, here.

Billy pulls parcel out jacket and hands to
Delilah who then snatched it from him.

                         BILLY (CONTINUES)
                    Geez, what's up with all the hostility?

                             DELILAH
                         Eat your food boy.

Delilah gets up and exits.

                                                  FADE TO:

INT. BROTHER HASSANS OFFICE - MIDDAY

Brother Hassan stands in his office with a
distinguished friend having a conversation.

                             HASSAN
                         So what do we do?

                             SENATOR
                Well without protest from the owners of these
                    properties there as good as gone.

                             HASSAN
                         How much for 2714?

                             SENATOR
                             3 million

                             HASSAN
                         Wow, just— David!

David walks in office lightly tapping on cracked open office door, he smiles and greats both men.

                DAVID
What's up brother Hassan; How are you doing sir? David.

The 3 men shake hands.

              SENATOR
Senator Williamston

                DAVID
Pleasure meeting you

              HASSAN
Excuse a moment Senator

              SENATOR
I was just headed out

The Senator exits the office, Brother Hassan sits at desk, David sits across from Brother Hassan

              HASSAN
David, what's going on man? Talk to me.

                DAVID
Just came back from the bank

              HASSAN
So you got that loan?

                DAVID
No, I seen Queen. This time for real. We spoke, I gave her my card so she can call me.

HASSAN
Your card so she can call you?.. your games getting weak bruh.

DAVID
Naw that's perfect, that's how I would want my wife to be, reserved, protectant and distant with strange men.

HASSAN
(Laughs) So what you gonna do when she calls?

DAVID
Talk to her.

HASSAN
Seriously? You've been talking about this woman for 10+ years non stop, and now that she's here I ask you what you gonna do when she calls all you can say is talk to her?

DAVID
I mean..

HASSAN
You mean what?

DAVID
Am I really supposed to come out with some corny shit like, "Hey Queen, I've liked you since we were 10 and that's why I walked you home everyday." Or something like " I started cropping extra hard to impress you."

HASSAN
Yes! Exactly like that.

DAVID

>   Brother Hassan you tripping!

>   HASSAN
> How? Telling a girl you started gang banging,
>   shooting at people, getting shot at all to
>   impress her is not corny. It was foolish as
> hell but most women would find that appealing.
>   On the other hand doing all that for a girl
>   and never saying anything, that's corny.

>   DAVID
>   Damn, I guess after all these years I wasn't
>   counting on actually getting the chance.

>   HASSAN
>   Now you got it, what are you going to do?

>   DAVID
>   I don't know

                                              CUT TO:

INT. WELTON ST. CAFÉ LATE AFTERNOON

Delilah is waiting for her food, she ignores a
call from a caller saved "$aint", Billy is
outside on the phone, a group of his friends
wait for him across the street outside on
Welton St.

                                              CUT TO:

EXT. WELTON ST. LATE AFTERNOON

Small group of friends pass a blunt around in
a semi circle.

>   CRIP HOMIE 1
>   Damn them mothafuckas clocking cuz

                        CRIP HOMIE 3
                          Who?

                        CRIP HOMIE 1
              This dispensary right here on the block

                        CRIP HOMIE 2
                        Duh mothafucka

                        CRIP HOMIE 1
                 That's basically a trap homie

                        CRIP HOMIE 3
                  It C like that sometimes cuz

                        CRIP HOMIE 2
         Who gives a fuck? You been acting real shareef
                    lately minister Farrakahn.

Everyone laughs.

                        CRIP HOMIE 1
                  Right, look, here come Billy now.

Billy strolls across the street to join his
friends, the greet each other with smiles and
3 daps each.

                           BILLY
                    Loved ones! Whats good?

                        CRIP HOMIE 2
                So what was T.C. talking about?

                           BILLY
                         What nigga?

                    CRIP HOMIE 1
                  What he say cuz?

                       BILLY
            He still on that bullshit with lowdown.

Disgruntled sighs and expressions from a few
members of the circle, one of the homies
notices David walking up Welton St.

                    CRIP HOMIE 3
            There go that nigga David right there.

                    CRIP HOMIE 2
           What he want us to do? Smoke the nigga?

                    CRIP HOMIE 4
                     Chill Cuz…

                    CRIP HOMIE 2
              I'll handle fam right now.

                       BILLY
               If you wanna die nigga…

                    CRIP HOMIE 2
              Damn cuz, it's like that?

                       BILLY
    Just watch yo mothafuckin mouth my nigga. I
    don't know what the hells a matter with this
                        guy.

Billy starts laughing and the rest of the
homies join in, Homie #2 doesn't join
laughter, he watches David as he continues up
the street and into Welton St. Café.

                                          FADE TO:

INT. WELTON ST. CAFÉ - LATE AFTERNOON

Delilahs speeds past David making her exit with food in tow, David shakes his head as she walks out, he has a smile on his face as he approaches the counter.

          DAVID
      Hey Janet!

Janet leaves from behind counter to give David a hug.

          JANET
      David! Hey!

          DAVID
    Have you seen mouse yet?

          JANET
He just walked in, he's in his favorite seat reading the paper.

          DAVID
     Bet, thanks Janet

          JANET
   You're welcome David.

David walks over to meet with Mouse who is currently reading the paper.

          DAVID
    What's up Mouse!

          MOUSE

David, have a seat my man, how you feeling today?

DAVID
I'm feeling alright man, how about yourself

MOUSE
I feel absolutely great David.

DAVID
Did you get a chance to check on those leads?

MOUSE
Yes.

DAVID
And…

MOUSE
They said no.

David looks away, frustrated and in disbelief

MOUSE
Hey man, I guess these urban development sponsors just-

David bangs fist on the table.

DAVID
This is bullshit cuz!

Mouse raises an eyebrow and seriously eyeballs David.

MOUSE
Cuz??

DAVID

                    This is bullshit man.

                         MOUSE
         Yea, but not a reason to relapse into
      cripping. We gone get ours, but if you bang on
         this mothafucking table again shaking my
       coffee and shit, you gone have some serious
                         problems.

They both laugh. David gazes out the window
and starts to have a flashback.

                                         FADE TO:

Black Screen 20 Years Ago.

14 year old Delilah, Kareem and David walking
up Welton St.
                         DAVID
        So where you tryna eat? Kaprees Chicken?
                        Zona's?

                        DELILAH
         Not Zona's I wanna sit down somewhere.

                         DAVID
                    Wings and things?

                        KAREEM
             I can get down with that!

                        DELILAH
                    Mmhhmm me too!

Billy comes walking up the street with to fist
full of gold rings and drapped in brand new
gear.

                         DAVID

Here come Billy, lil baby shocca! What up cuz!

>   BILLY
>   What up low down, what up krazy k cuz?

>   KAREEM
>   What up B.S. loc?

They all laugh, Billy not so much

>   DAVID
>   Hell naw, B.S. loc.

>   BILLY
>   I'm just billy I keep telling yall

>   DAVID
>   Yea sure you right Billy loc, you hungry?

>   BILLY
>   Where ya'll tryna eat?

Billy pulls a large wad of money out of his pockets

>   KAREEM
>   Damn cuz where you get all that?!

>   DELILAH
>   For real Billy!, What?!
>   BILLY
> I been with T.C. all day hustling while ya'll
>   been at school.

>   DELILAH
>   You got all that in one day?!

>   KAREEM
>   These rings and shit real?!

BILLY
Hell yea

DAVID
Hustling what? The same thing yo mom smoke? Everybody already know T.C. be fucking on yo mom...

Billy looks away in despair

DAVID
Look my bad cuz, I just don't like that nigga man.

KAREEM
Yea I don't trust cuz neither.

BILLY
Yea, so ya'll tryna eat or what?

DAVID
Hey yo Kareem, there go your pops people.

A Brother from the Nation Of Islam walks up the street with goods for sale, Kareem hides his blue rags when he sees the Muslim Brother.

BRO KAHLIL
As salaam Alaikum Brotha Kareem.

KAREEM
Walaikum salaam sir.

BRO KAHLIL
David.

DAVID
What's cracking cuz?

Delilah and Billy snicker with each other

          BRO KAHLIL
Young lady do your parents know where you're at?

David wraps one arm around Delilah shoulder

          DAVID
I am her parents, brotha…

          BRO KAHLIL
Really?

          DELILAH
Yes, really!

          BRO KAHLIL
I see

          BILLY
Look man, how much for one of those pies?

          BRO KAHLIL
3 dollars young brotha

          BILLY
Let me get 2, and one of those papers.

          BRO KAHLIL
7 dollars young brotha

Bro Kahlil's eyes double when Billy pulls out his wad of cash again.

          BRO KAHLIL
Well that's a lot of money young brotha, do you know what to do with that?

                         BILLY
           Yea, keep the change. have a good one brotha,
                        we out ya'll.

Billy walks away, and the other kids follow,
David is the last to move taking the moment
all in as the Muslim brother puts away his
money.

                       BRO KAHLIL
           May Allah bless you for your aid to the
                         messenger!

                                              FADE TO:

INT. 715 - NIGHTFALL

The four kids sit eating and conversating at a
table piled with food.

                         BILLY
           I don't know why you so tight about T.C.
                  anyway, homie like you cuz.

                         DAVID
             I don't think about that nigga man.

                         BILLY
           And you don't need to. Think about the money,
              and the mothafucking spread we eating.

                        DELILAH
                      For real tho.

Delilah attempts to high five Billy, he
doesn't high five back, he shoots David a look
with his eyebrow raised. Kareem starts
speaking with his mouth full.

KAREEM
We don't fuck with that nigga T.C., this here crippin about family, that nigga T.C. all about self.

BILLY
Family huh…

DAVID
Yes, family mothafucka, you got a better one?

BILLY
Im gonna get this money.

KAREEM
Don't froget locked up, like the rest of the homies that followed cuz.

BILLY
And, honestly I don't give a fuck, yall should be more thankful.

DAVID
What nigga!? Fuck this food cuz!

David stands up and throws his plate on the floor.

DELILAH
Low Down you trippin!

DAVID
No bitch you tripping

DELILAH
Bitch?!?

DAVID

Yea, bitch! What you don't think I see you eyeing cuz this whole time we eating, you want this lil nigga?

David gets mad and storms off. Kareem still eating with his mouth full

                    KAREEM
              So we out cuz?!

                    DAVID
            No, I'm out, cuz…

David exits the restaurant, Billy gets up to go follow him.

                    WAITRESS
       Who's gonna pay for this mess?

                                FADE TO:

INT. BILLY'S CAR - LATE NIGHT

David coughs as he, Billy and Kareem smoke a blunt in Billy's car.

                    BILLY
          Hit that shit then

                    DAVID
            Right on cuz

                    BILLY
Yea I already know, I'm glad you decided to roll… real shit Delilah needs to focus up. Her nose wide open, she don't got no business even being over here, if you don't turn her out someone else will, on the game.

                    KAREEM
              Let me hit that
                    BILLY
My bad cuz… this what niggas need to be on,
riding getting high and getting this money,
for real us 3 together riding tough til the
                wheels fall off.

                    KAREEM
              I'm with that cuz!

                    BILLY
             What about you David?

                    DAVID
I'm with this, I ain't selling no dope tho.
I'd rather ride on some mothafuckas than
                   slang.

                    BILLY
                  Oh yea?

                    DAVID
                  Yea nigga

                    BILLY
              I got you homie.

Billy gives a devilish grin.

                                        FADE TO:

EXT. OUTSIDE BILLY'S CAR FACING FRONT THROUGH
WINDSHIELD - AFTER DARK

Billy's headlights are off as he David and
Kareem sit in the car and conversate
inconspicuously.

BILLY
There they go right there

KAREEM
I see them niggas cuz

BILLY
Shh! These mothafuckas be strapped too, we gone get as close as we can and start dumpin, they gone have dope and money. We gone rush these taco eating mothafuckas get what we can and be ghost. Ya'll down?

KAREEM
I'm down cuz

DAVID
You tripping cuz, you too K-Rock

BILLY
You said you wanted to ride on some foos

DAVID
If im a catch my first body, it's gonna be for some shit that count!

BILLY
Nigga this do count, you gona get paid, and you ain't gotta sell no dope.

KAREEM
C'mon cuz

DAVID
Cuz…

BILLY
Fuck it, we gotta move out now.

Billy opens his glove box and reveals 2 twin 9mm pistols, he hands one to Kareem, he then pulls a .40 caliber handgun from the side of his seat. He looks at the other pistol in the glove box then makes eye contact with David.

                    BILLY
          C'mon K-rock, we out…

Billy and Kareem exit the car.

                                        FADE TO:

INT. SHAHIDS APARTMENT - MIDDAY

Fashback within a flashback, David sits on living room couch, Shahid is standing up holding a gun chastising David in full FOI uniform.

                    SHAHID
     Listen to me David, taking a life can be a
       serous offense when done unjustly. I'm not
     going to take your weapon away from you, but I
        do want you to understand it and the power
                       that it holds.

Shahid hands David his gun, and David shakes out of his flashback to Kareem opening Billy's rear driver side door.

INT. BILLY'S CAR - AFTER DARK

                    KAREEM
    Yea nigga wake up! We ain't even have to shoot
         nobody, we on nigga! Shit was crazy!
                      (BOOM!)

Kareem is shot in the head,

CUT TO:

PRESENT TIME

EXT. IN FRONT OF 715 -

The gun blast shakes David out of flashback, he is standing on Welton St. a lightrail train speeds by.

FADE TO:

EXT. 5 POINTS - EARLY EVENING

David walks to Brother Hassans office, he knocks on the door,

CUT TO:

INT. INSIDE T.C'S CONDO - EARLY EVENING

T.C. opens his door for Billy.

              T.C.
            My man!

             BILLY
Ay loc, I gotta be straight up with you, I support buy back the block, and as soft as David done got I support the nigga him and Brother Hassan.

             T.C.
First of all don't be barging up in my shit with all tis fucking noise, secondly what's your mothafucking point?

             BILLY

                    I'm just sayin homie-
                              T.C.
Just saying? That's not your job homie. Look
around all that fake ass political shit, buy
back the block… this ain even the hood no more
   loc, all the niggas in Green Valley Ranch.

                            BILLY
  Straight up homie the locs ain't riding on
                       this one.

                             T.C.
      Why? Is it because you won't make them?

                            BILLY
  Nigga why the fuck would niggas smoke David
 and sabotage some positive shit in the hood,
                   that's for us!

                             T.C.
 Look Billy, I taught you a lot, I helped you
   become who you are today, a general in my
  army. You get money, you got all the clout,
    and there were things done and things that
  still need to be done to maintain that. Some
  of these things are beyond your scope of the
  imagination… I need you to be the leader how I
                   taught you to-

                            BILLY
    Look I said what I said , I'm out cuz

                                         CUT TO:

INT. BROTHER HASSAN'S OFFICE - EARLY EVENING

David sits in front of Brother Hassan's desk
as the two wrap up a casual conversation.

                    HASSAN
Man, that is disappointing, but we will find a
       way, we got to keep believing that.

                    DAVID
          Yea, what else is there

                    HASSAN
We just keep grinding, do what we can do for
        now. Can't stop won't stop.

                    DAVID
                    Right.

                    HASSAN
I know it's hard to stay positive, and faith
may be all we have, but you'd be surprised at
  the works that come from having big faith.

                                    DISSOLVE TO:

INT. DELILAH'S HOUSE - EARLY MORNING

Music combines with the sound of food being
cooked, Delilah sits down to eat breakfast,
dressed to impress completely flawless. She
takes a bite of food and spits it out.

                    DELILAH
        Did you put milk in these eggs?

                    JASON
    Only a little, you can't even taste it.

                    DELILAH
              Actually I can.

Delilah gets up to throw the rest of her plate
away.

DELILAH
I told you about making me this nasty ass shit.

JASON
Damn babe don't throw all that food away.

DELILAH
I bought the shit.

JASON
What that got to do with wasting it?

Delilah slams dishes in the sink.

DELILAH
Mothafucka when you start handling things around here let me know… you got my appetite fucked up, I need to go get something to eat.

JASON
The kids is sleep still…

Delilah grabs her purse, rushing out.

DELILAH
I know, that's why I said I! need to go get something to eat.

JASON
Wow.

DELILAH
Wow what!?

JASON
Nothing fam

Delilah rolls eyes and laughs

DELILAH
I'll be back.

CUT TO:

INT. LUCEROS RESTURANT - MORNING

David enjoying himself on a breakfast date with Queen.

DAVID
Seriously I was glad to see your text, it took you a week, but its cool, today you made my day.

QUEEN
Aww that's sweet, (laughing) why is that?

DAVID
It's just good to catch up with an old friend.

QUEEN
Old friend huh?

DAVID
I thought we we're friends. What brings you back to town anyways?

QUEEN
My grandmother needs some help around the house, I can take my work with me so I came. I kinda wanted to see what all the hype was about too, you know I haven't been back since like '93

DAVID

Yea, its definitely a completely different town looking back to then, very few things left. Our community pulled right from under our feet at such a great time to be on the points.

QUEEN
Ok Malcom X, I see you. So what did David Low Down Brown grow up and become?

DAVID
I started a non profit for young boys without fathers, we have classes available 7 days a week, focusing on entrepreneurship group economics and trade skills. Lately that's taking the back seat to my buy back the block initiative, I'm thankful for my team.

QUEEN
Really… you know I'm on to you right?

DAVID
On to me?

QUEEN
Yea, on to you, you good at too…

DAVID
What are you talking about?

QUEEN
This whole nice, perfect, polite role you're playing just to get in my draws…

DAVID
Excuse me?

QUEEN

You know how you guys do, I'm just an acquisition on your checklist that you haven't got a chance to mark off. You coming at me with this love jones crap, looking at me like you miss me, hoping I look back into those pretty brown eyes as if I just seen forever, as if you been thinking about me this whole time after all these years.

DAVID
Wow, you really got it all figure out. I guess.

QUEEN
Negro please… we're grown. And what you men need to realize, is women have their own hit list too! So not only would the straight up approach be more successful, it's preferred.

DAVID
Preferred?

QUEEN
Yes preferred, I mean it's cute meeting for breakfast and all but let's be real, are you going to say after all these years a relationship with me has been on your mind? Pleeease don't be that type.

DAVID
Type?

QUEEN
Oh, the type to be out here grown as hell still advertising a relationship just to get some booty…

DAVID

Wow, this conversations really going left.

QUEEN
YEA..

Queen checks her watch, she starts getting her things together and standing up.

QUEEN
Speaking of left, I got to go, sorry. I only had enough time for coffee, the Lucero's tho. Bomb.

Queen stands up. David stands up.

DAVID
I see…

QUEEN
Yea, thanks again.

DAVID
Here I'll walk you to your car.

QUEEN
How kind of you.(laughter)

CUT TO:

INT. DELILAH'S CAR PARKED ACROSS FROM LUCERO'S - MORNING

Delilah checks herself in the mirror and notices David walking Queen to her car, she watches him go back in the restaurant.

DELILAH
What the fuck?... is that Queen?? And with David?

Delilah sprays herself with perfume. Queen drives away allowing Delilah a better view.

DELILAH
Wow that really is Queen, little chocolate girl all grown up. Look at David's silly self, he know he still want this.

CUT TO:

INT. LUCEROS RESTURANT - MORNING

David is ordering more food and see's Delilah walking his way coming into Lucero's. David is obviously impressed, but also annoyed by Delilah's presence.

DAVID
Here we go.

DELILAH
Hey David, Mr. save the hood.

DAVID
Right…

DELILAH
Ugh, I was giving you a compliment, I actually think what you're doing is really good.

DAVID
Well I apologize.

DELILAH
Apology accepted. I wanted to talk to you about how I could help.

DAVID
Really?(in disbelief)

                    DELILAH
        Yea, really, maybe we could meet up later or
                      something..

                     DAVID
                    Delilah…

                    DELILAH
        What? You think I'm coming on to you?

Delilah steps into David.

                     DAVID
        Here's my card, leave me a message on my
                    office line.

David grabs his drink and leaves.

                                            CUT TO:

INT. DAVID'S CAR - MORNING

David gets into his car after leaving Lucero's, before he starts driving he starts receiving text message notifications.

                 TXT MSG:DELILAH
        You really tried to front on me in front of
           them bitche sin Lucero's… it's cool tho.

                 TXT MSG:DELILAH
        You know you still love me, I was your first
                 and you were mine lol.

                 TXT MSG:DELILAH
             I really do miss you David.

                 TXT MSG:DELILAH

                  Let me take you to dinner, we can go eat some
                        Ocean Prime, something really good.

                              TXT MSG:DELILAH
                         Hit me back when you not busy.

David almost crashes looking at texts.

                                                   CUT TO:

INT. DELILAH'S HOUSE - NOON

Jason is on the couch smoking and spying on
Delilah's text thru her ipad, kids making
noise in the background.

                                   JASON
                 Wow.. really bitch!? Wasn't even a fucking
             virgin, fucking bitch! I fucked my whole life
             up behind you bitch! Thirsty ass trifling ass
               hoe! Y'all kids shut the fuck up!... c'mon
                 Jason , you can't keep doing this shit to
             yourself man, bitch run around doing whatever
                 she want, don't even break bread… these
             probably ain even my kids… that's probably why
             none of the homies respect me, I was supposed
             to be in the NBA, off track fucking with this
             bitch… I told y'all kids shut the fuck up!...
                     That's it im coming with my belt!

Jason explodes to his feet and starts to yank
off his belt.

                                                   CUT TO:

INT. DAVID'S BATHROOM - EARLY EVENING

David removes his belt and sits his phone on
bathroom sink before getting in shower. Once

in the shower David starts receiving text messages again.

                    TXT MSG:DELILAH
                  What you think of this?

Delilah sends a sexy picture of herself in lingerie. David checks his messages and sees her picture while still in the shower, he puts his phone back down without replying.

                    TXT MSG:DELILAH
           Its rude to ignore someone you know, your read
                         receipts are on.

                                                  CUT TO:

INT. DAVID'S BEDROOM - EVENING

David fresh out the shower entering bedroom, checks phone, sends Queen a text message.

                    TXT MSG:DAVID
                         Hey.

                    TXT MSG:QUEEN
                         Hey…

                    TXT MSG:DAVID
                  Did you make it home safe?

                    TXT MSG:QUEEN
                My home is Alabama, Bye David.

                                                  CUT TO:

INT. BROTHER HASSAN'S OFFICE - EVENING

Queen sits across from brother Hassan's desk, he is going over some information with her, she is distracted by her cell phone.

> BRO HASSAN
> Excuse me young lady?

> QUEEN
> Sorry Uncle Cory.

Hassan clears throat.

> QUEEN
> Uncle Hassan. (laughter) it's just this guy… this kid, I grew up with. I'm trying to let him down easy.

> HASSAN
> What's his name?

> QUEEN:
> David. He's doing the whole passive aggressive role and you know I don't do beta males.

> HASSAN
> (laughter) I see… are you talking about David Williams?

CUT TO:

INT. DAVID'S KITCHEN - NIGHT

David is making himself something to eat, he checks his phone.

> DAVID
> Nope. Not even gonna respond to that.

Another message comes thru, attached is an ass shot from Delilah.

     TXT MSG:DELILAH
 Can I see you please, I really need to see you..

     TXT MSG:DELILAH
Look, maybe the pictures is doing too much. But what is you on?

     TXT MSG:DELILAH
    Can we at least talk?

     TXT MSG:DELILAH
   Where you at right now?

David stands in the kitchen reading the messages as they come in, thinking hard if he should reply, he slips into a flashback of Shahid lecturing him about immoral women.

        FADE TO:

INT. SHAHIDS LIVING ROOM - AFTERNOON

Shahid stands lecturing a young David who sits on his living room sofa.

      SHAHID
 So that's the young woman you choose?

      DAVID
     What?

      SHAHID
  She's worse than the last one.

      DAVID
    Here we go…

SHAHID
Listen to me David, the only thing more dangerous for you right now than these streets, is an immoral woman. Pay attention to the lessons in the scripture, all her paths and all her ways lead to death… I've already lost one son.

David explodes to his feet.

DAVID
What?! I lost everything before I even had it!

SHAHID
Don't! raise your voice in this home again.

DAVID
You don't gotta worry about that, I'm out.

David pivots and is headed out the door.

SHAHID
David. I love you son. Remember what I told you about the spirit. It's just heavy on my heart to tell you to be careful with these little girls. Especially the ones that SEEK attention, they will never be satisfied, they seek you out, consume you, until they possess your very life. And still they will not be satisfied. Our women are so beautiful, gifted, talented, each and everyone of them special. But in this wilderness we have learned to disregard these things and I see it getting worse. These little girls don't value themselves so they can't value you. Allah is the only man they need right now, he made you so attractive so you could bring them back to

him. The messenger teaches us she may seem sweet like honey-

DAVID
Shahid! I'm out…

CUT TO:

INT. DAVID'S LIVING ROOM - NIGHT

David sits on his sofa, looks at his messages and decides to reply to Delilah.

TXT MSG:DAVID
I'm at home.

TXT MSG:DELILAH
I'm free right now, send me the address and I'll be on my way.

David shows hesitation before he reluctantly sends his address

TXT MSG:DAVID
3415 High St.

TXT MSG:DELILAH
See you in a minute.

CUT TO:

INTERCUT - INT. DAVID'S LIVING ROOM/ EXT. WELTON ST.

David is relaxing for a few moments then he receives a call from Queen.

DAVID
Hello?

Queen is smiling from ear to ear walking down the street. She and Billy pass each other, the two do not recognize each other.

                    QUEEN
                Hey, David

                    DAVID
                What's up?

                    QUEEN
      I feel like such an idiot.

                    DAVID
                Really..

                    QUEEN
Yes, you didn't know brother Hassan was my uncle.. and he told me everything.. well, I've always felt the same way.

The both laugh and smile.

                    QUEEN
        Can I come see you?

                    DAVID
              Of course.

                    QUEEN
     Cool, text me the address.

                    DAVID
                  Ok.

                    QUEEN
   Alright, see you in a minute.

                    DAVID

> Alright.

They both smile and laugh as they hang up. Soon after David remembers that Delilah is already on her way to him.

> DAVID
> Oh shit, Delilah.

David calls Delilah.

> DAVID
> Hey Delilah, we should do this another time, something came up.

> DELILAH
> Well it's gonna have to wait.

> DAVID
> Yea, I mean… hold up, what?

> DELILAH
> You heard me, it's gonna have to wait.

> DAVID
> No-

> DELILAH
> I'm on your porch David.

David goes to open his front door, his jaw drops when he sees Delilah in sexy lingerie, she pushes him in the house, a sex scene takes place in the front room.

> FADE TO:

INT. DAVID'S FRONT ROOM - LATE NIGHT

David wakes up on sofa, he finds a note left behind by Delilah who has already left. David goes and takes shower, while in shower he texts Queen.

TXT MSG:DAVID
Sorry I'm just getting a chance to get back to you, I couldn't cancel my previous plans and got tied up.

TXT MSG:QUEEN
Understandable, do you have time to meet tomorrow?

TXT MSG:DAVID
Yes! I have a few errands then we can get together for a late lunch, early dinner?

TXT MSG:QUEEN
Cool, you have somewhere in mind?

TXT MSG:DAVID
Welton?

TXT MSG:QUEEN
Ok

TXT MSG:DAVID
I'll call you when I'm 30 minutes out.

TXT MSG:QUEEN
Sounds good!

FADE TO:

INT. BILLY'S ROOM - EARLY MORNING

Billy sits on his bed with an old shoe box, he is looking at pictures , he pulls out a blue bandana that used to belong to David, he also has a picture of himself, David and Kareem when they were younger.

CUT TO:

INT. BROTHER CALEB'S BARBERSHOP - EARLY AFTERNOON

Brother Caleb's barbershop is in full swing, barber chais are full and as usual the barbers are leading a friendly debate.

              BARBER 1
I don't mind what they doing down there on the Eastside. For real, niggas had all the opportunity to do something with it. Instead of all this moaning and groaning we need to do something with Green Valley Ranch before you niggas be crying about losing that next.

              BRO CALEB
Don't be disrespectful to all the things we have done right here on the Fax and the Eastside. I'm talking about Zona's , Pig Ear Stand, 715, Wings and Things, Kaprees Chicken-

              BARBER 1
Okay! And most of that shit is gone, and so is most the niggas. So why we tryna buy back the block?

              BRO CALEB
It's prime real estate, right near downtown easy access to I-25&I-70, not to mention we have a long history of making it what it is today.

              BARBER 2

Well Green Valley is close enough to the Airport, you see DIA expanding too.

BARBER 1
Then they put that resort out there.

BARBER 2
Exactly, Green Valley is prime too! Why not move forward?

BRO CALEB
My question to you both of you brothas is, what type of investments have y'all made in Green Valley? And brotha you don't even live there.

BARBER 1
That's not the point, we as a people gotta start being more proactive and less reactive.

BRO CALEB
True indeed. But until you brothas are doing more than "moaning and groaning", as you like to call it, I rest my case.

David walks into the barbershop with a proud stride.

BRO CALEB
Brother David! As salaam-alaikum

DAVID
Wa-laikum salaam sir

The two embrace in a familiar NOI greeting, David then works the room starting with Barber 1

DAVID

What's up brotha?

                BARBER 1
             What's up nigga?

David gives a telling look before extended his hand for a handshake.

                DAVID
       How you doing today brotha?

                BARBER 1
                Good-

David puts the barber in a wrist lock in the blink of an eye.

                DAVID
If you ever call me nigga again, I'll be sure to let you meet him. You hear where I'm coming from?

                BARBER 1
               I gotchu!

                BRO CALEB
Ok, that's enough, David let me talk to you outside.

Brother Caleb and David exit the barber shop.

                              CUT TO:

EXT. IN FRONT OF BARBERSHOP - NOON

David stands side by side laughing with brother Caleb.

BRO CALEB
Now that was funny.

DAVID
You know I don't even trip like that but bruh had it coming for a minute now.

BRO CALEB
Hey, he deserved it.

DAVID
You remember when you taught me that lock?

BRO CALEB
First month training to be one of the mighty FOI

DAVID
Good times, I had to make sure I could still use it.

BRO CALEB
You know the brothas could use YOU still..

DAVID
I haven't gone anywhere, I'm you know, reverse cointelpro on this whole thing, so to speak.

BRO CALEB
Right, you come for that money right?

DAVID
Yes, yes sir

Brother Caleb has clearly become displeased by their conversation. He jabs a envelope into David's chest.

BRO CALEB
Here it is, you know where to find me.

Brother Caleb attempts to walk away.

> DAVID
> Hey, you know its all love with me and the brothas.

> BRO CALEB
> I know brotha David, we love you too. Now get outta here before Denver's finest think we're making a drug deal.

> DAVID
> As-salaam Alaikum

> BRO CALEB
> Walaikum salaam

Bother Caleb goes back in shop leaving David outside

FADE TO:

INT. DELILAHS LIVING ROOM - MIDDAY

Jason sits on couch smoking a blunt, when Delilah busts in the door with excitement.

> DELILAH
> Mommy's home!
>
> JASON
> The kids is sleep

> DELILAH
> Why the hell the kids always sleep?

> JASON
> Yea fuck all that bullshit bitch.

                    DELILAH
                    Bitch?!

                     JASON
      Yea bitch, I know exactly why you ain come
                 home last night.

Jason shows Delilah the i-pad with her text
thread with David on screen. Delilah smirks
and laughs at him.

                    DELILAH
      Wow, you really are so fucking weak. And you
      the bitch… really nigga? And you wonder why my
      pussy don't get wet for you… Look, while you
        spying on me and shit I suggest you start
         filling out job apps and look for somewhere
      else to stay. And some prayer might be a good
            idea, I got yo bitch, bitch ass nigga.

                                         DISSOLVE TO:

INT. BROTHER HASAN'S OFFICE - MIDDAY

Brother Hasan sits at his desk looking over
paperwork, Billy rushes in office, drops a
bank roll on Hasan's desk, he is in a rush to
leave back out.

                     HASAN
                 Billy my man!

                     BILLY
      What's up Brotha Hasan, here's those ends I
                promised. I gotta go.

                     HASAN
            Alright little brotha, be safe

                    BILLY
               You too!

                                        CUT TO:

EXT. FOLLOWING DELILAHS CAR - MIDDAY

Delilah drives down the street, smile on her
face reminiscing of last night with David.

                                     DISSOLVE TO:

INT. UPSCALE RESTURANT - MIDDAY

A well dressed, dark looking man sits alone
drinking a glass of champagne wearing lightly
tinted steel frame glasses. Delilah walks in,
when she spots the man she joins his table.

                    DELILAH
               Hi baby.

                    SIR L'S
               How you doing love?

                    DELILAH
          I'm good, sort of having a rough day.

                    SIR L'S
               Oh no, what happened?

                    DELILAH
          Jason called me a bitch today..

                    SIR L'S
          Hold up, so you want me to go smoke yo baby
                         daddy?

                    DELILAH

Well, no. it's not that deep, um-

SIR L'S
No listen baby, don't do that. Next time it better be that deep, don't be having my blood hot for no reason.

DELILAH
I'm sorry baby-

SIR L'S
That's what you get for having that weak ass niggas kids and then marrying him anyway, mr. basketball (laughs).
You really thought you was gonna be a NBA wife, that ain even shit. Delilah! What you thinking about? I'm talking to you… Who you been fucking girl? I see it all on you, somebody got you in yo feelings.

DELILAH
Naw

SIR L'S
Look Sir L's ain tripping off all that, I knew the day I picked you up walking, I knew you was gonna be a million dollar hoe, but even then you still wanted that fantasy love shit, that's not for you, you too real for that baby. You better learn from this nigga that's your baby daddy now. Money over everything.

DELILAH
I already know daddy, it's not-

SIR L'S
Aht! Just go get that money at table six.

Delilah gets up heading to table 6, as she passes Sir L's grabs her arm.

                    SIR L'S
                Aye, real love

                    DELILAH
                Real love.

                                        FADE TO:

EXT. COMMUNITY EVENT SITE - LATE AFTERNOON

David gets out his car and stands in the middle of a destroyed set for his community event. He is in despair that gradually changes to rage. He cries in rages, he notices tags sprayed from his old hood.

                                     DISSOLVE TO:

EXT. WELTON ST. - LATE AFTERNOON

David spots Billy and his crew, he storms in their direction striping his tie, and rolling up his sleeves. David's approach causes some of the homies confront David, he meets them with violence first.

FIGHT SEQUENCE BEGINS
David is eventually brought to his knees with a punch to the gut and head. Billy cocks his gun back to freeze everyone.

                    BILLY
      Enough! What the fuck is going on here?! The
            fuck wrong with you nigga!?

                    DAVID

>   Fuck you Billy.

>   BILLY
>   Oh you was coming for me?

>   DAVID
>   You a coward homie, I know you trashed my
>   event.

>   BILLY
>   Cuz without me you wouldn't even have an
>   event, you need to get yo mind right before
>   you fuck around and get smoked.

>   DAVID
>   You gone kill me cuz?

>   BILLY
>   Nigga get yo ass up.

Billy puts his pistol away, David stands up.

>   DAVID
>   I'm not yo nigga.

David tries to deliver a haymaker to Billy, but is caught with a knockout blow to the side of his head. The knockout send him in a flashback to Kareem's funeral.

>   FADE TO:

INT. FUNERAL HOME 25 YEARS AGO - MIDDAY

Young David sits in pew with a blank star on his face. Young Billy comes and sits next to him.

>   BILLY

I'm sorry cuz, I know Kareem was a brother to you, he was a brother to me too, it happened tho cuz. Kareem would want us to be strong, I'm your brother too cuz.

Billy pulls out a polaroid picture of David, Kareem, and himself when they were younger.

BILLY
Y'all was both the only family I got… look at the picture low down. You all I got left. On crip cuz I'd give my life to make sure you keep yours and that's forever cuz, on the game. You hear me cuz? Low down you hear me? David? David? David?...

FADE TO:

INT. BILLY'S LIVING ROOM - LATE EVENING

David is sleep on Billy's sofa, wakes up to his name being called, Billy is making tea in the kitchen he jumps when he sees Billy.

BILLY
You alright cuz?

DAVID
What happened?

BILLY
You almost got stomped to death, you's a wild boy. Here drink this.

DAVID
What is this?

BILLY

It's chamomile, peppermint and ginger. This mix will be good for you right now.

DAVID
So you a doctor now?

BILLY
I've been into pharmaceuticals all my life, natural and designer.

They both laugh a little. Billy sits in chair across from David.

BILLY
Seriously tho bruh, I love you cuz. It sucks we haven't really talked in years and it comes to this. I love the eastside as much as you do, but times have changed, we don't got the same leaders we had when we was kids and that just real.

DAVID
So you ruin my event?

BILLY
I already told you it wasn't me.

DAVID
Ain nobody stupid enough to fuck with anything on this side of town unless your hand in it. They fear the consequences too much, only people ain scared of you is the police.

BILLY
On my momma I ain do it.

DAVID
So who did it Billy?

Billy stands up, he answers the question while going back into kitchen.

BILLY
I don't know.. look cuz you got bigger fish to fry, because throwing a buy back the block event for awareness but this ain't the hood no more. What you need to do is get ya money up and get your head in the game. I know. You think I'm just out here hustling and playing all day, but I got a couple M's put up, you could have the same. Remember Delilah? Of course you do, she gotta be touching about mil too. Shit probably more, she be out here on some renegade shit, I know it!

DAVID
Prostitution?

BILLY
Yea selling pussy, getting the chalupa… wait? Oh hell naw cuz you been hitting that? Damn what happened? I thought no adulterer goes unpunished?

DAVID
I ain't BEEN hitting that.

BILLY
It's all good cuz, only reason I don't fuck with her is because of you, check this out.

Billy opens a shoebox on the kitchen counter and pulls out a blue bandana and throws it to David. He also pulls out a polaroid picture that he takes with him to sit next to David on sofa.

DAVID
This my shit huh?

BILLY
Yea check this out, I never let go homie. Even though you push me away you the only real family I got,

David looks at the picture of Billy, Kareem and himself, it's the same picture from the funeral flashback.

BILLY
And that's why I gotta tell you, you can't come down here no more.

DAVID
What??

BILLY
Look, niggas want you dead.. and.

DAVID
From that shit today?!

BILLY
Hell naw, look my hands is tied on this one, honestly it gots me thinking about leaving the game altogether. Shit ain't making sense no more.

DAVID
It never did, that's what I was always trying to tell you.

BILLY

What else did we have? What niggas was supposed to go to college be doctors or some shit?

DAVID
Shit was fucked up, but when you change the way you look at things the things you look at will change.

BILLY
Yea uh huh, that's real cute (laughter) I guess we should both go join the army and shit (more laugter)

DAVID
Ok you got jokes.. oh shit Queen.

BILLY
Queen?

David frantically looks for his phone, Billy hands it to him from the arm of the couch.

DAVID
Yea, from back in the day.

BILLY
Back in the day, Back in the day?? I think I seen baby girl. She was looking right too! You hitting that?

DAVID
Man shut up fool (laughs)

BILLY
My bad playa (laughter)

DAVID
Hey Billy I gotta skate.

BILLY
Alright, I had the homies park your car downstairs.

DAVID
Already cuz

Billy makes a silly face shooting David an eyebrow

BILLY
Uh huh.

DAVID
Shit, haha

BILLY
For life!

DAVID
Yea I guess, just don't call me nigga again

BILLY
Already, Already (laughter)

The two shake hands and hug, David exits

BILLY
(To himself) Be safe LowDown

CUT TO:

INT. T.C'S CONDO LIVING ROOM - LATE EVENING

Delilah stands in a mirror putting her lipstick on, T.C. comes out of the bathroom looking revived and relieved.

                        T.C.
Damn girl, you really are the best in the
west. The way you was sucking my dick tonight
made me think it wasn't even mine no more.

Delilah rolls her eyes in mirror.

                      DELILAH
            Thank you, I'm flattered..

                        T.C.
When can I see you again? I want the same
                   performance.

                      DELILAH
     I don't know, I'm thinking about retiring.

                        T.C.
Well here's your money, 5 rackereths, plus a
little extra. You know help you reconsider
                 early retirement.

Delilah rolls her eyes and reaches for money,
T.C. pulls the money back.

                        T.C.
                   Aht aht aht.

T.C. purses his lips out for a kiss.
                      DELILAH
                      Really?

                        T.C.
          Don't be acting brand new.

T.C. places a finger on his lips to make the
target clear for Delilah, she gives him a
small kiss and takes her money.

                    T.C.
               See you later.

                    DELILAH
               Whatever nigga.

                              FADE TO:

INT. DAVID'S LIVING ROOM - LATE EVENING

David lays in Queens lap on his sofa while she tends to his bruises.

                    QUEEN
               I still can't believe you.

                    DAVID
               What?

                    QUEEN
     You're too old to be fighting, really, you all
                    need to grow up.

                    DAVID
               I am grown up

                    QUEEN
               I can't tell.

Queen submerges David's hand in ice water.

                    DAVID
          Ahh shit, you could've just kissed it.

                    QUEEN
          You want me to kiss it huh.

                    DAVID
            Or you can just kiss me

They kiss.

                                        CUT TO:

INT. BROTHER HASSANS OFFICE - MORNING

Brother Hassan stands waiting in his office more casually dressed than usual. Billy comes in unsure of what's going on.

                    BRO HASSAN
              Have a seat Billy.

                    BILLY
              What's going on?

                    BRO HASSAN
        You tell me, why did you have those kids
              destroy our set up like that?

                    BILLY
              What?

                    BRO HASSAN
        Don't lie to me son, you know I know about
        everything happening over here. Especially
              when it involves our babies

                    BILLY
        Well, did you know there was a hit out on
                        David?

                    BRO HASSAN
        I heard about it, I heard you had his back
                        too.

BILLY
Well this shit is above me, if I let David do that event yesterday I mine as well have pulled the trigger myself.

BRO HASSAN
Are you serious?

BILLY
I know everybody think I got control over all the homies but that's not always the case.

BRO HASSAN
Does T.C. have anything to do with this?

BILLY
T.C.?

BRO HASSAN
Billy, don't come in my office and try to make a fool of me. Is T.C. behind this whole thing?... I'm not mad at you brotha, I know secrets too, sometimes I wonder if it's all the secrets that hold us back… I owe you an apology, you'll understand later. I'm gonna get to work on this thing, I heard about the brawl yesterday, is David okay?

BILLY
Yea he's good, with his new woman right now. I seen her leaving here a few nights a ago..

BRO HASSAN
My niece, Queen. Let's pray and work to keep David safe for her sake.

BILLY
Already.

                    BRO HASSAN
                Thanks for coming to see me.

                       BILLY
                      Anytime.

Billy stands up, he and Bro Hassan shake hands. Billy exits.

                                        FADE TO:

INT. DAVID'S LIVING ROOM - AFTERNOON

David lays in Queens lap asleep. A text message comes thru on David's phone, it's from Delilah. Queen ignores at first, but decides to look when multiple messages come thru.

                   TXT MSG:DELILAH
                    Hey boo, WYD?

                   TXT MSG:DELILAH
            I'm still wet from the other night
                   TXT MSG:DELILAH
             Are you home? I wanna come see you!!!

David wakes up, Queen places his phone back.

                       QUEEN
         Yea, you might wanna get that, excuse me.

Queen throws David up out of her lap and storms away angry. David just woke up and is confused.

                       DAVID
                    What the hell??

QUEEN
Right! What the hell David? You stood me up to fuck Delilah?

David hangs his head low with protest.

QUEEN
Bye David.

DAVID
Queen hold up, it's not like that.

QUEEN
What's it like? All this black community self-righteous shit is just a act, you just like every other nigga.

DAVID
Look don't call me a nigga, I'm sorry ok. Will you please sit down?

QUEEN
No, I'm sorry too. Bye David

Queen leaves, David I upset and he calls Delilah.

DAVID
Delilah, I apologize for what happened the other night, because it was a mistake. And I don't wanna see you no more.

DELILAH
Well hello to you too. You trippin boo, is it that little bitch Queen?

DAVID
Hey, all that's unnecessary

                        DELILAH
          Don't tell me how to talk nigga, you ain't
          nobody to tell me how to talk, with the ame
          mouth you ate this pussy with. When yo dumbass
                  figure the shit out call me nigga.

                         DAVID
             Delilah I don't want nothing to-

Delilah hangs up phone in David's face.

                                                CUT TO:

INT. DELILAH'S CAR - LATE EVENING

Delilah puts her phone down frustrated, starts talking to herself angrily.

                        DELILAH
          This stupid ass, fake ass Martin Luther King
          ass nigga! He really gone make me fuck this
                        little bitch up.

                                               FADE TO:

INT. DAVID'S KITCHEN - LATE EVENING

David at home calling both Delilah and Queen frantically, getting no response so he text back.

                      TXT MSG:DAVID
          You gotta believe me about the other night,
          that was the first time I've hung out with
              Delilah in over 20 years. I made a big
          mistake, by the time I talked to you she was
                   at my door. Please forgive me…

                                               FADE TO:

INT. BAR - LATE EVENING

Queen is sitting at the bar with her girlfriend Tasha having a drink.

                    TASHA
          Damn girl who blowing you up like that?

                    QUEEN
                    David.

                    TASHA
          Fine ass David from the eastside? Mr. fight
                    the power?

                    QUEEN
                    Yea, him.

                    TASHA
          Ooh girl, that nigga is fiiine.. what you
                    gonna do with that?

                    QUEEN
          Nothing, I ain't thinking about that man, he
                    ain nothing special.

                    TASHA
          I can tell (rolls eyes knowingly)

                    QUEEN
                    Shut up.

                    TASHA
          For real, why you tryna be low? He blowing you
          up like that, what the hell ya'll got going
                    on?

QUEEN
I said nothing!

TASHA
Don't seem like nothing, personally I thought the nigga ws gay?

QUEEN
Uh-uh girl (both laugh)

TASHA
For real girl, he don't talk to nobody! Never seen him on a date never heard of him having a girl. Shit, I even tried to throw him some and he turned me down

QUEEN
Tasha?

TASHA
What? If he blowing you up like that you must've really put it on him. (Tasha laughs)

QUEEN
Naw you got all wrong, him and Delilah be creeping.

TASHA
Delilah??

QUEEN
Yea Delilah.

TASHA
Girl hell naw! I doubt it, them two are like water and oil

QUEEN
I seen her texting him.

TASHA
Damn...

QUEEN
Yea I know what I'm talking about.

TASHA
Well that's strange.

QUEEN
mm-hmm

TASHA
For real, my best friend Tanisha baby cousin Robin invited me to her god sister birthday party and Delilah was there, we was all talking about different guys from back in the day and David's name came up. She was talking about how glad she was she didn't lose her virginity to such a weak man and how one weak man was enough for a lifetime. She started bragging how she stole him from some other girl. The bitch is crazy, for real if you ask me she get off on breaking up happy homes, that's how she got wound up with Jason as her Baby Daddy, everybody know that.

QUEEN
I gotta go make a call.

As queen turns to get up from her seat, Delilah walks in, Tasha pulls Queen back down

TASHA
Ooh shit girl, speak of the Devil.

As Delilah approaches the bar Queen is staring her down.

DELILAH
Excuse me? Do I know you??

Queen notices her benz keys in her hands.

QUEEN
Hmm, you drive a blue Mercedes s-class?

Delilah starts inching her way towards Queen, Queen gets out of her seat and gets behind it to make sure there is space between her and Delilah.

DELILAH
Um yes I do.. so-

QUEEN
So you do know me, and you were parked outside of Welton St. Café when I was on a date with my man.

DELILAH
Your man?

Tasha gets up and gets in between Delilah and Queen

TASHA
Is everything ok here?

QUEEN
Just fine, I was just telling Delilah how my man has been blowing me up all night waiting on me to come back. He slipped and fell in some garbage a few nights ago, I had to leave because it still STUNK.

Queen breezes by Delilah with that last remark, she and Tasha are exiting. A few on lookers catch Delilah's attention.

                    DELILAH
 Yea whatever bitch! It ain't stink when I was riding the niggas face bitch! Don't get fucked up while you back in town little girl!

Queen stops and turns around.

                    QUEEN
            Delilah, grow up.
Queen and Tasha continue their exit.

                    QUEEN
  Let's stop somewhere else, I need another
                    drink.

Tasha waves bye to Delilah teasingly.

                              FADE TO:

INT. DAVID'S LIVING ROOM - AFTER 2AM

David sits on his couch heavily stressed, he checks his messages to find Queen still hasn't text so he calls, she doesn't answer. David's doorbell rings, he opens his door and it's Queen obviously tipsy holding out her cellphone.

                    QUEEN
  I hope you don't plan on blowing me up like
         this every girls night out.

                    DAVID
                    What??

Queen throws herself around David and kisses him passionately, this leads to the two making love.

                              FADE TO:

INT. DAVID'S BEDROOM - AFTER 2AM

David and Queen making love.

                           DISSOLVE TO:

2 MIN LOVE SEQUENCE THROUGH SUMMER

                              FADE TO:

INT. HAIR SALON - MIDDAY

Delilah's Hair is under they hair dryer and she's reading a magazine. Other customers are in the shop talking.

                    TAMICA
    I'm just saying girl you don't gotta put up
    with all that, there are good men out there
    you just gotta put yourself where there at.

                    NIKKI
     You right, I really do think I'm done with
    niggas tho, might need to broaden my horizons.
                    TAMICA
    Now I ain saying all that, I wouldn't even
          know what to do with a pink man.

Several of the ladies in the shop laugh.

                    NIKKI

Uh uh. I ain't going that far, but some of these Mexican men..

TAMICA
Girl..

NIKKI
Especially the ones that grew up with us. Remember Alex Martinez?

TAMICA
Fine!

NIKKI
Fine, Fine!

TAMICA
Remember him and David at the parties back in the day?

NIKKI
Ooh David! That's the one.

TAMICA
Yea he Boo'd up now.

NIKKI
What? Well somebody got lucky.

TAMICA
That's what I'm saying girl there are good BLACK men still available.

NIKKI
Yea whatever, who he with now anyways?

TAMICA
Her name is Queen, my sister said she from here, stayed on the Eastside back in the day.

NIKKI
Hmm. I ain never heard of her.

TAMICA
Yea she David and them age. My sister said she checked Delilah little bougie ass so hard behind her man.

NIKKI
What?

TAMICA
Yea this was a few weeks back tho. This nigga David is a trip my sister tells me everything ok girl be telling her.

NIKKI
What you mean?

TAMICA
He's just perfect, treating ol girl like a straight Queen.

Delilah is Fed up, she jumps from under the hair dryer.

DELILAH
Excuse me, but before you get to gossiping about other people's business and shit make sure they not around.

Delilah storms of her hair isn't finished.

HAIRDRESSER
Dee! Your hair!

DELILAH
Fuck this ghetto ass shop, I'm going somewhere else!

Delilah exits.

DISSOLVE TO:

EXT. PARK BBQ EVENT - MIDDAY

David and Queen casually walk through the park bbq event. Many children and other adults are in attendance.

                  DAVID
I hope they don't take all day on the grill.

                  QUEEN
          Right, me either.

An older woman approaches David for a hug.

               MRS. BROWN
Hi David! Glad you could make it out.

                  DAVID
Hey Mrs. Brown, its good to see you too! This is my girlfriend Queen, Queen, this is Mrs.
                  Brown

            QUEEN/MRS. BROWN
Nice to meet you. (the two laugh)

               MRS. BROWN
(still laughing) really it is nice to meet you, nice to finally see David with a woman on
              his arms.

                  DAVID
                Hey now.

MRS. BROWN
David now you know I'm telling the truth, Ms. Queen, I hope you really do live up to your name because this is a really special young man here. I remember just last spring we had a big storm, knocked down several fences in the neighborhood. David was the one to get a few guys together and had all those fences up and brand new within a week! Ok?

QUEEN
Thank you Mrs. Brown, I'm very aware of the man I'm with and who he is, I hope he recognizes who he's with. Because Queen, that is definitely who I am. If you could excuse me for a moment, I need to refresh my drink.

Queen winks at David and sashays away. Mrs. Brown is impressed she and David watch her walk away.

MRS. BROWN
Ooh David, that's a bad one you got there.

DAVID
Right on. Mrs. Brown im 37 now, how long you gonna refer to me as young man?

MRS. BROWN
Well I'm 67 so what is your point exactly?

DAVID
You know what, I'm not even gonna play with you today.(laughter)

MOUSE
Yo low down!

David turns to see mouse approaching him, he's happy to see him, the two embrace.

MOUSE
Whats up with you King David?

DAVID
What up mouse?!

MOUSE
Let me holla at you real quick. How you doing Mrs. Brown?

MRS. BROWN
Very well, thanks for asking.

David steps off to the side with mouse.

DAVID
So what's good Mad

MOUSE
You tell me love bird.

DAVID
I see you got jokes.

MOUSE
Yea and in the words of the great Rakim I ain one. And neither is my time or energy.

DAVID
Mouse what the hell are you talking about?

MOUSE
I'm talking about you Don Juan, you fell in love and I haven't seen you at the tables, you gave up on the community event everything just

>   stopped. My time end energy was invested in
>   all this too. So what's the deal?
>   DAVID
>   I'm taking a break.
>
>   MOUSE
>   Ain't no breaks, this is what we live for,
>   can't stop won't stop. You been by to check on
>   Roy? I already know you haven't, but you
>   should. He's sick man, it's pretty bad I know
>   he'd love to see you.
>
>   DAVID
>   Alright I'll go check him out.

                                                        FADE TO:

EXT. OUTSIDE ROY'S APARTMENT - LATE AFTERNOON

David knocks on Roy's apartment door, a nurse eventually answers.

>   NURSE
>   Who is it?
>
>   DAVID
>   David Williams.

After a few moments the nurse opens the door.

>   NURSE
>   Hello?
>
>   DAVID
>   Hey, is Roy home?
>
>   NURSE
>   Right this way.

David follows the nurse to Roy's bedroom. Roy is watching the television, he turns it off the moment he sees David.

>   ROY
>   David!

>   DAVID
>   Hey Roy, how are you sir?

>   ROY
>   "How are you sir?"?-
>   What's up brotha?

>   DAVID
> Not too much, I heard you were sick so I'm
>   checking on you.

David has a seat across from Roy.

>   ROY
>   Oh, you checking on me huh?

>   DAVID
> Yes sir, I know I haven't been by all summer
>   and all.

>   ROY
>   Well, here I am!

David and Roy have a laugh.

>   DAVID
>   Right, so what's new?

>   ROY
>   What's new with you?

>   DAVID
>   Not much really, same old-

ROY
Wait a minute, not much really? Last I heard you was damn near married. Oh you ain think I heard about that? Does she not share your values or have your views changed? Did you give up? What's going on brotha?

DAVID
Well it's deeper than that.

ROY
How so?

DAVID
Well some people don't like what I'm doing and will go as far as to kill me to stop me.

ROY
So now you're making progress.

DAVID
I don't know.

ROY
I remember back in '64, Dr. King came to town. Back then we had barricades through our communities preventing us from traveling certain roads, back when the eastside was actually the eastside because that was the furthest east most of us were allowed to travel. Did you know there was a point and time they wanted blacks confined to this part of town? Well King came and changed all that, to this day white folk only talk about the speeches he gave at DU, but I seen it myself Dr. King right here on the Eastside in 1964 with the National Guard in tow.

I got close enough to Dr. King to catch wind
of him receiving death threats while he was
here. When he was assassinated 4 years later I
could only imagine he received death threats
everyday until that day. It wasn't until years
later when I had got a few death threats of my
own that I understood why he kept going and
the way he did. The assignment we've took part
in takes a life's sacrifice, it's not for us,
its for the future. You know at one point
today was yesterday's future, and you can
decide what tomorrows looks like.
I'm blessed to have seen the results of King's
efforts, even more blessed to have been part
of it.

              DAVID
Wow, I had no idea, that's amazing.

               ROY
      Oh you think so?

             DAVID
Yes, you really put some things into
        perspective.

               ROY
Yea man, so who's the girl?

                               CUT TO:

INT. T.C. CONDO - LATE AFTERNOON

T.C. hands Detective Mier a drink before
fixing one for himself.

             DT MIER
  Queen, that's her name.

                        T.C.
Boom, there you go that's it. Like I said he's
been running around with this girl all summer,
    look Billy handled David we don't have to
              worry about him no more.

                      DT MIER
Oh he handled him alright, I would think by
now you would understand how all this works.
After 25 years you would think you'd get it
when I give orders that's exactly how they
              should be carried out.

                                        CUT TO:

INT. ROY'S BEDROOM - LATE AFTERNOON

Roy stands up.

                        ROY
    You can't be distracted, you're far too
valuable. A woman? Death threats? Is that all
          it takes to knock you off course?

INTERCUT - ROY'S ROOM/ T.C.'S CONDO - LATE
AFTERNOON

                      DT MIER
    The only reason half these blacks are even
    here is because the '76 Olympic games that
                  never happened.

                        ROY
You were born for this, you can't let anything
remove you from your assignment. You David!
              You! You are so special.

                    DT MIER
Yea everyone thinks there so special, news
flash you're not, we're all apart of the same
machine. In fact you guys are the garbage we
 throw in the incinerator to keep this engine
                running (laughs)

                      ROY
 It's not funny, I'm serious the same energy
  king had I see that energy all over you. I
don't want you to lose your life, but what is
     your life if you stop fighting.

                    DT MIER
 All this black power, kings and queens, gods
  and goddesses bullshit, I don't see it. J.
Edgar hoover was one of those ignorant scared
whites. A black messiah from the ghetto coming
 to unify these monkeys. Can you believe that
                     shit?
                      ROY
J. Edgar Hoover, the first director of the FBI
  launched an entire government operation on the
   voice of the black man and woman, don't ever
     underestimate the power of our voices.

                    DT MIER
Listen Too Cool, we've been doing this for a
 longtime, we grew up in this shit, together,
  like brothers. But if we so much as here a
     peep out David's fat ass mouth you're
   finished. And I'll kill the fucking nigger
                    myself.
                                      CUT TO:

EXT. INFRONT OF ROY'S BUILDING - LATE
AFTERNOON

David stands staring off in front of Roy's building when Mr. B walks up.

MR.B
David what's up man?

DAVID
Oh hey Mr. B, how you doing?

MR. B
I'm good, I haven't seen you in awhile.

DAVID
Yea, I was just visiting with Roy, he was telling me about Dr. King visiting in '64.

MR. B
Oh yea David, it went down man. Before king was here, back in the 50's they'd arrest me just for crossing York, just for being black.

DAVID
Wow, you know what Mr. B I gotta take off, it was good seeing you.

MR.B
Oh fasho David.

FADE TO:

INT. DAVID'S HOME - EARLY EVENING

Queen is in the kitchen preparing a meal, David comes storming in the house looking for her.

DAVID
Queen, Queen!

QUEEN
I'm in the kitchen baby.

DAVID
Hey beautiful.

David places a gentle kiss on Queens lips.

DAVID
What are you making

QUEEN
Hey baby, nothing yet, I'm washing this lamb for later.

DAVID
Sounds good.

QUEEN
Uh-huh, so what's wrong with you?

DAVID
Nothing… well I went to see an old friend of mine, Roy Seymour. He's kind of on his last leg

QUEEN
Oh, I'm sorry to hear that?

DAVID
Yea, over the years I've kicked up a lot of dust with Roy, he would come down to the jail and visit me when I was fighting my case. He was the one who got me motivated to make a difference in my community.

QUEEN
Was this the same gun case you took for Billy?

DAVID
Same one, junior year.

QUEEN
So he's been a mentor of yours for a quite a while.

DAVID
Yea, I gotta get back on my horse babe. People are counting on me, and believe that I can make a difference. You gotta understand baby I love you, but this is where my heart is, this is my passion.

QUEEN
I'm excited for you babe.

DAVID
Really?

QUEEN
Yes! I know the community is your passion. That's the only reason I decided to have my job transferred back to this hicktown.
(laughter)

DAVID
Oh you got jokes huh?

David pulls Queen in for another kiss.

QUEEN
You know something else?

DAVID
What?

QUEEN

That was the first time you told me you love me. And, I love you back. (kiss)

DAVID
Don't start nothing, won't be nothing (kiss)

FADE TO:

INT. DAVID'S LIVING ROOM - NIGHTFALL

David and queen lay together naked under a small blanket on the living room sofa, David is awaken by his phone ringing.

DAVID
Billy what's up bruh?

BILLY
Yo David you sleep cuz?

DAVID
Yea man, everything ok?

BILLY
Yea man, I wanted to link up with you cutty, what you doing tomorrow?

DAVID
Linking up with you.

BILLY
Bet, call me when you get up, I'll be up.

DAVID
Alright.

BILLY
Gone.

FADE TO:

EXT. 715 PATIO - EARLY MORNING

Billy sits down eating breakfast, David walks up and joins him.

> BILLY
> What up wit it D?

> DAVID
> Good morning bruh, how you feeling?

> BILLY
> I feel free.

> DAVID
> That's what's up.

> BILLY
> Well, I'm almost free. I'm moments away from walking away from all this. I just wanted to talk to you first.

> DAVID
> Now that's what's up for real right there.

> BILLY
> No for real for real, over the last 3 months I got custody of all 3 of my sons, I got a cool little spot ducked of in AZ. I'm leaving in a few weeks.

> DAVID
> You serious?

BILLY
Dead serious.

DAVID
Wow, that's amazing.

BILLY
I wanted to talk to you g, because you the only family I got. And I love you g.

DAVID
I love you too bro.

BILLY
You know this one of the last times you'll get to say I told you so.

DAVID
What you mean?

BILLY
I mean everything, look around. We've lost so much to gain so little.

DAVID
Yea, I watched it happen, and the fact I was a part of it makes my life's work right here.

BILLY
What you gonna do now?

DAVID
I'm throwing a rally downtown, I'm just looking for fresh energy. Then I'm jumping right back in where I left off. I'm headed to make these flyers soon as I leave from with you.

BILLY

Let me fund that, as a going away present.

                DAVID
                Bet.

David reaches for a pound.

                BILLY
       Fasho, but I meant right now.

Billy pulls out a large bag of money,

                BILLY
           This you g.

                DAVID
           What's this?

                BILLY
It's yours homie, I'm doing everything I plan on doing immediately. Tomorrow's not promised today, I finally get the meaning. You know tonight's the anniversary for Shocca.

                DAVID
       I usually keep track

                BILLY
Yea, well breakfast is on me too. I got a few loose ends I want to tie up.

                DAVID
         Already homie

The two shake hands, Billy passing money and locking C's with David.

                BILLY

For life.

FADE TO:

INT. T.C. CONDO - EARLY MORNING

A loud banging at the door causes T.C. to put out his blunt and get up to see who it is.

          T.C.
Man who the fuck is this banging on my mothafucking door this early in the got damn morning!

          BILLY(From outside the door)
          It's Billy homie.

T.C. opens the door and sees Billy who smoothly walks right in.

          T.C.
Man nigga what the fuck you want that can't wait.

          BILLY
I just want to get at you man to man about me leaving all this shit alone.

          T.C.
Nigga what the fuck is you talking about?

          BILLY
This nigga.

Billy throws small duffle bag full with money on the floor.

          BILLY

                    To make shit fair, because ain none of the
                              homies replacing me.

                                      T.C.
                    (starts laughing) nigga you could've just
                              left, who the fuck is you?

                                     BILLY
            I'm the nigga that made shit happen, I put in
                         the work I called the shots-

                                      T.C.
                    Bah! No one wants to hear that shit.

T.C. heads over to his bar cart to make a
drink.

                                     BILLY
       But you gone hear me tho, you may think you
    made me but I am me. I'm baby shocca, you know
              who my big homie was. Or you forgot?

                                      T.C.
         Look I don't know what all this shits about
         cuzzin, straight up. R.I.P. to the locs, but
                   you gotta make that shit plain.

                                     BILLY
    Nigga I see you for who you are, the devil in
    disguise. You are a destroyer, this wasn't a
    bad neighborhood until I helped you make it
                                      one.

                                      T.C.
    (laughing) woah, pretty harsh words. So that's
      why you sympathize with David, well who's
         gonna protect him now that you're gone?

                                     BILLY

The same person who always has, God.

T.C. throws his head back with laughter.

                    T.C.
     Ohh shit! Now I'm up! Thank you father for
           another day and another drink.

T.C. plants himself on his sofa to enjoy his 2nd drink.

                   BILLY
     I'm leaving this money in good faith that I'll
     never have to hear from you again, im washing
     all ties and connections with you today. Look
        at you, pathetic, slithering, heartless,
                         wicked-

                    T.C.
                   Billy.

                   BILLY
              What?.. What?

T.C. hears Shocca's voice echo "what?" and again a second time.

                    T.C.
                 Nevermind.

T.C. hears two gunshots go off in his mind.

                   BILLY
                 I'm out.

When Billy exits and closes the door a 3rd gunshot goes off in T.C.'s mind.

                              DISSOLVE TO:

25 YEARS AGO

EXT. SPEER BLVD - AFTER MIDNIGHT

Young T.C. and Shocca leaving a party walking along the Hudson River.

SHOCCA
Man that party was live

T.C.
I told you, you seen them girls.

SHOCCA
Man baby girl in them Red Biker Shorts, now that's my type of hype.

T.C.
I told you these parties be jamming man, that one little click from around the way was even in there.

SHOCCA
Yea homeboys only I seen that, Michael Tipton was in there too! All the ballers in they broncos trucks. Shit was tight.

T.C.
There was some other people at the party too.

SHOCCA
Duh nigga.

T.C.
Ok, but I'm talking bout some important people.

T.C. pulls out a package with drugs in it.

SHOCCA

>   What the fuck is that cuz?

>   T.C.
>   What you mean what is it?

>   SHOCCA
>   Nigga I know what it is, but what's that got
>   to do with me?

>   T.C.
>   Damn that's how you acting? The homies could
>   eat off this.

>   SHOCCA
>   Not homies from my hood, niggas a sell some
>   bud, but that crack shit got niggas moms and
>   whole families out here fucked up.

>   T.C.
>   So niggas ain't tryna eat?

>   SHOCCA
>   I got the keys, and we ain't having it. It's a
>   million ways to get this money.

>   T.C.
>   Where I'm from the homies all slang, we can
>   really get rich off this, who said because we
>   in the streets we gotta struggle.

>   T.C.
>   Like I said, this my hood and we not rolling
>   like that, now excuse my back.

Shocca turns his back on T.C. And walks a few feet away to take a piss.

>   T.C.(to himself)
>   Damn shame, I thought you had what it took.

T.C. Puts his package away, and pulls out a revolver.

                    T.C.
                Say Shocca!

                   SHOCCA
                   What?!

Shocca turns his head around to see T.C. With his gun drawn.

                   SHOCCA
         What the fuck is you doing Cuz?!

T.C. Shrugs his shoulders and fires 3 rounds into Shocca.

                                    FADE TO:

INT. DELILAH's LIVING ROOM - MORNING

Gun blasts from Grand Theft Auto rang out in sequence with the gun blasts that kill Shocca. Jason is playing the video game and smoking a blunt.

                    JASON
      Damn cuz, I'm always getting peeled at the
      same fucking spot! Fuck this game… oh shit, is
              that my nigga Billy outside?

Delilah comes walking out from back room to see out the window.

                   DELILAH
              Damn that was fast.

Delilah goes to get her bag out the room and then proceeds to go outside. Jason of course watching like a hawk.

> JASON
> Hey what's Billy doing pulling up over here?

> DELILAH
> I don't know hold up.

Delilah walks out the front door, Jason eventually peeks out behind her.

> BILLY
> Hop in the car tho!

Billy and Delilah share a inside laugh.

> JASON
> Billy bad ass what up cuz?

> BILLY
> What up sidah, you good?

> JASON
> A-1, you good? I heard what happened with that mark David, on the set I'm a drop cuz when I see him.

> DELILAH
> What?!

> BILLY
> What the fuck you just say nigga?

> DELILAH
> No nigga you tripping. You need to go in the house

JASON
Billy hold up.

BILLY
Dee hop in the car. Watch out fam.

Delilah gets in Billy's passenger seat.

JASON
Aye homie, I ain't-

BILLY
Watch out right quick Jason.

Jason takes a few steps backwards, Billy rolls up his window. Billy moves his shirt so Delilah can see the pistol on his lap.

BILLY
What the fuck is yo Baby daddy talking about?

DELILAH
I don't know this nigga gets weirder day.

BILLY
So I should handle his weird ass now then.

DELILAH
Nigga not in front of my house, the kids in there and everything.

Billy rolls his window down. Jason starts approaching the car. Billy spits out the window in Jason's path.

BILLY
Aye cuz, on my dead homies rest in power, you better watch yo fucking mouth cuz. You don't know what you talking about for one, and you

ain't no factor out here my nigga. You couldn't even see my nigga LowDown, yous a has been hoopstar that didn't make it.

Jason now extends his hand in apology.

JASON
My bad, I was tripping.
Billy does not shake Jason's hand.

BILLY
Naw just think before you speak, now I'm a holla at yo BM and I'm a get at you.

JASON
Alright fam, I'm inside baby.

Jason goes in the house. Billy watches him mad as hell

BILLY
Clown.

DELILAH
Ugh! Anyways, what's up, what's so important?

BILLY
I'm done Dee, I'm outta here.

DELILAH
Boy what are you talking about?

BILLY
Look before I leave I wanted to give you something.

Billy pulls a gift box from the side of his seat.

DELILAH
what's this?

She opens it and pulls out a nice retro diamonds and gold tennis bracelet.

BILLY
it's a tennis bracelet, I got it when they was still popping bout 20years ago.

DELILAH
What?? This is nice, so why you giving it to me.

BILLY
Because it's yours, I bought it for you back then, you know I had a crush on you too hard back in the day. You know why I never crossed the line too.

DELILAH
Damn Billy.. you really been getting this money for a long time.

BILLY
Man.

The both share a laugh.

BILLY
For real tho Dee, you my best fucking friend in the whole world.

DELILAH
Billy stop, you bout to make me blush.

BILLY

                        Oh shoot.

Billy makes a funny face and dance. Delilah
laughs.

                        DELILAH
                   Billy stop playing.

                         BILLY
    No but for real I wanted you to have that
   bracelet because it means something different
                       to me now.
   So much has changed, but you've always been
    the same, the same person today as you were
             yesterday for 25 years straight.

                        DELILAH
                   Damn, that's dope.

                         BILLY
   On the game. That bracelet is us locked in for
   life, me and the kids bout to shake to AZ. I'm
              a miss you the whole time.

Delilah throws herself around Billy and gives
him a kiss on the check.

                         BILLY
   Ok now, don't start nothing won't be nothing.

                        DELILAH
                     Shut up Billy

Billy extends his pinky, like a pinky promise.

                         BILLY
                        4 life.

                        DELILAH

4 life.

FADE TO:

ONE WEEK LATER

INT. DAVIDS KITCHEN - AFTERNOON

David is in the kitchen talking to queen while she is cooking.

QUEEN
That's so amazing, I'm happy for Billy and the kids they all look just like him!

DAVID
Crazy right, they're good kids too, just like Billy was.

David's phone rings.

DAVID
Let me get this.. Hello. This is he. Grandmother? No I don't have a grandmother. Well of course, I was a orphan. Really? Ok I'm on my way..

QUEEN
Um, what's the deal? What's going on?

DAVID
A woman related to the cousins is on her deathbed and claims I'm her grandson.

QUEEN
What??

DAVID

                    Yea, I don't know what this is about, but I'm
                         gonna run and go check it out.

                                   QUEEN
                    Ok I'll have dinner ready by the time you get
                                    back.

                                   DAVID
                                Thanks Babe.

David gives Queen a kiss then exits.

                                                    DISSOLVE TO:

INT. HOSPITAL HALLYWAY - LATE AFTERNOON

David is scanning the floor looking for the room that could hold his grandmother. When he finds the right room and looks in he sees the older black woman who came to his school so many years ago, of course the woman is older now. David has a brief flashback to that day in the office. He snaps to quick.

                                   DAVID
                         So you were my grandmother?

                                   DOCTOR
                            Mr. David Williams?

                                   DAVID
                    So why did you just leave me like that?

                                   DOCTOR
                    Excuse me sir, are you David Williams?

                                   DAVID
                              Yes that's me.

DOCTOR
Your grandmother is under a lot of pain and stress that we can not see.

DAVID
Yea me too.

MS. COUSINS
Young man.

David turns to see the old woman pointing behind him, it's a well dressed Jewish man who knocks on the already open door before letting himself in.

Ben
Hello, Mr Williams I presume?

DAVID
Yes.

BEN
Nice to finally meet you, my name is Ben Ackermann I am your grandmothers Attorney.

DAVID
Ok, so maybe you can tell me what's s actually going on?

BEN
Sure, right with me David.

David follows the lawyer out of the hospital room into a waiting room.

BEN
When Ms. Cousins asked me to look up your medical records I couldn't find anything prior to the age of 4, which was very unusual, not

even a birth record. David what is your date of birth?

DAVID
August 1st 1980

BEN
That's interesting, because my client believes you're David Cousins born August 8th 1980, and your mother was Clarissa Cousins. Now deceased.

DAVID
What a surprise.

BEN
None of this sounds strange to you?

DAVID
Of course it does.. but it sounds true too.. as far as I knew I never had a family. I was born under a rock.

BEN
Well David if you give us consent and we find a match on a paternity test between you and Ms. Cousins. That's gonna be an extremely valuable rock you were born under. Are you prepared to take the test today?

DAVID
Wait what?

BEN
Ok, I know it's a lot to take in. Quite frankly Ms. Cousins has been fighting to hold on, the last several months she's been nom stop with determination to find you. It sounds like you haven't had the easiest life, with a match today your life is going to change

dramatically for the better. I'm talking 6figure shareholders, million dollar bonds dozens of properties residential and commercial.

                    DAVID
Properties? Wait, is this Elizabeth Cousins?

                    BEN
So you know your town history, yes the last heir of the wealthiest black family to ever reside in Denver Colorado. Her family, or your family I could say –

                    DAVID
I'll take the test. Just give me a moment.

                                        FADE TO:

INT. DAVID'S CAR – LATE EVENING

David sits in his car in the hospital parking garage talking on the phone with Queen.

                    DAVID
Yea it's amazing. But I feel empty inside. I don't know what to make of all this.

                    QUEEN
I understand babe, I can't believe she knew who you were all this time.

                    DAVID
Right, and now she dies with all the answers to my questions. This shit ain't right, it's not fair.

                    QUEEN
I hear you baby.

DAVID
NO! this is bullshit!

QUEEN
David calm down.

DAVID.
What did I do? Huh? What the fuck did I do? I ask for this shit.

QUEEN
Right, but you still got it. Babe I know you better open your eyes and see that you're blessed. Look what you just told me this woman left you behind. You can really do all that you ever dreamed of. What she did leaving you at that school was cowardly, but she robbed you of nothing. So what she didn't take you in. The little David I knew didn't wanna be inside or follow no rules no way.

David laughs to that.

DAVID
Hell naw, you right. That shit just hurts.

QUEEN
I could only imagine, but I know you can handle it.

DAVID
Thanks Babe.

QUEEN
Of course boo, I'm here for you. I was gonna run to the store right quick are you coming straight home?

                    DAVID
    Yea, yea, you know actually let me swing by
    Brother Hassan's and then I'll be there.

                    QUEEN
                    Okay.

                    DAVID
               I love you baby.

                    QUEEN
              I love you too.

The call ends, David prays.

                    DAVID
    Dear God, I'm tired. Help me see this through
    to the end, calm my emotions and guide my
    thoughts lord so that I may not fail. All tho
    I feel vast down I lift you up in praise for
    you are the best knower and may your will be
               stronger than mine. Amen.

David calls Hassan.

                    DAVID
    As Salaam Alaikuim.. Brother, can you show me
                how to make a will?

                                            FADE TO:
INT. T.C.'s CONDO - EARLY MORNING

Detective Miers knocks on T.C.'s door, no
response so he knocks some more.

MIERS
Come on Mr. Too Cool it's time to wake up! I gotta show you something! I know you're in the there!

After a few moments a still tired T.C. Answers the door in his bathrobe.

MIERS
There he is.

T.C.
What the hell is going on, it's early as fuck.

Detective Miers let's himself in brushing past T.C.

MIERS
Last time I came here, I believe I told you if we heard heard one peep from David you're done right? Right?

Detective Miers throws a flyer down on T.C.'s coffee table.

MIERS
Well there he is, peeping like a motherfucker.

T.C. Doesn't look at the flyer he goes to his bar cart and makes a drink.

MIERS
What you don't wanna look at your hero all clad in black power on his little flyer.

T.C.

>   Look man just get to the point, I'm getting
>   tired of hearing all this bullshit before you
>   get to the point.

Detective Mier nonchalantly has a seat on
T.C's sofa

                         MIERS
> The point is your done T.C., finito, finished,
> fried! You really fucked this one up. Check
> this out, our little David Williams, LowDown,
> is actually David Cousins. Oh you don't know?
>   The little fucking nigger is loaded, and now
>   he owns half of the commercial property in
> 5points. Yea, this rally of his is tomorrow,
> where he probably plans on announcing the news
>   to the "community" we can't let that happen.
>   Now you see, we have to handle this
>   ourselves.. T.C. You have 24hrs to get the
>   hell out of dodge, all your accounts are
> frozen, properties seized, vehicles in process
>   of repossession as we speak. I know you
>   recently started having a distaste for cash,
>   but you're welcome to take any cash on hand
>   with you. Buy you a ticket.

                         T.C.
>   Miers, you can't be serious.

T.C. Sits his drink down, goes to get his
phone and checks his accounts, he sees the
accounts are empty.

                         MIERS
>   It's gone T.C. all of it.

                         T.C.
>   So what the fuck am I supposed to do?

                    MIERS
Don't tell me you don't have any money now?

                    T.C.
         What about my fucking life?

Detective Miers let's out a big sigh, then gets up from the sofa.

                    MIERS
I would say sorry, but I'm not. Over the last 40 years you've helped move nearly $5Billion dollars worth of product.

                    T.C.
            That shit wasn't easy.

As Detective Miers speaks he inches towards T.C.

                    MIERS
You got to wear the hottest clothes, have sex with beautiful women, have nice things, pretend you're a fucking king and all on tax free money. If you ever established something for yourself we would've took it, but you didn't even try.

Miers now faces T.C. face to face.

                    MIERS
Here's another newsflash for you, you little monkey! You wanna hate me right now, but hate your fucking self, you and all the rest of them.(sigh) Enjoy the rest of "your life" T.C.

Detective Miers exits, a single tear rolls down T.C.'s face.

                              FADE TO:

TOMORROW

INT. DAVID'S BEDROOM - MORNING

David wakes up and smells breakfast is ready, almost instantly Queen walks in carrying a tray of food.

                    QUEEN
          Good morning Mr. Cousins!

David shoots her a quizzical look.

                    QUEEN
          Too soon?

David smiles.

                    DAVID
          No you're good.

Queen sits the food tray across David's lap.

                    QUEEN
          You ready for the big day?

                    DAVID
          Yea, yea

                    QUEEN
          Is everything ok?

Queen sits on bed next to David.

                    DAVID
Yea, it probably just hasn't hit me yet how real all this is. I feel like I've just been going through the motions all week, and today feels like it could last forever.

                    QUEEN
Well between David Williams-Cousins community rally, and Billy Clarence going away party today just might last forever.

They both laugh.

                    DAVID
I hope not.

They laugh and kiss.

                              DISSOLVE TO:

INT. DELILAH'S LIVING ROOM - MORNING

Clouds of smoke fill the room Jason is smoking with a friend of his. He's holding up one of David's flyers and used the blunt to burn David's eyes out.

                    JASON
Yea fuck this nigga, bitch ass nigga fake as hell! Heal the hood and all this pro-black shit. I'm a smoke this fake ass nigga cuz.

                    KEITH
Damn you sound like a hater. (Laughs)

                    JASON

Real shit nigga, this mothafucka been fucking my wife and shit.

                KEITH
This nigga David?

                JASON
Yea nigga, this nigga right here. And I'm a smoke this nigga.

Jason throws Keith the flyer.

                KEITH
At the rally? You sound dumb as fuck, what you gonna smoke him with you ain't strapped.

                JASON
Oh so you think you know me.

Jason pulls out gun from couch cushion.

                JASON
Uh huh, niggas gone learn today.

                KEITH
Nigga you hot! At the rally tho?

                JASON
Man hell naw, ain't gone be no rally. Watch this.

Jason pulls out iPad.

                KEITH
The fuck?

                JASON
Nigga pay attention.

Jason shows that he is typing a text message to David as Delilah.

                              CUT TO:

INT. DAVID'S LIVING ROOM - MORNING
David is sitting on the sofa having a glass of wine.

                    QUEEN
          I guess it's never to early for wine.

                    DAVID
               How was your prayer?

                    QUEEN
          Great, I needed it. I started to feeling a
            little funny after our talk earlier.

Queen joins David on the sofa.

                    DAVID
          You sure that was from the talk or is it that
                   somebody maybe coming.

David rubs Queens belly.

                    QUEEN
          You better stop playing, this month number 2 I
                     missed my cycle now.

                    DAVID
                    Hey, my bad

                    QUEEN
          Yea, so you should hurry up and marry me.

                    DAVID
            No problem, let's do it right now.

                    QUEEN
    Um I may be seasoned, but I still want a real
                  wedding David.

                    DAVID
        Say less, we'll do it at the rally.

                    QUEEN
       David stop playing, and just answer your
            messages or something please.

Queen gets up from the couch laughing, goes to pour a glass of wine.

                    DAVID
               I'm for real why not?

David starts to read messages. You can see him unease, and his mood drops. Queen notices

                    QUEEN
                Baby what's wrong?

                                        CUT TO:

INT. DELILAH'S LIVING ROOM - MORNING

Jason sits back waiting on a text response still smoking with his friend. He damn near jumps out his seat when he sees David's read receipt

                    JASON
      We got action! Yea he reading the shit right
                       now.

                    KEITH

                    Aye I'm out homie.

Keith gets up to leave. Jason points his gun at him.

                         JASON
          Sit yo black ass down, you in to deep now.

                                          CUT TO:

INT. DAVID'S LIVING ROOM - MORNING

Queen and David sit on the couch David is very frustrated and stressed, Queen is very much concerned.

                         QUEEN
               So she's lying right? Right David?

                         DAVID
                    Fuck! I don't know.

                         QUEEN
               Wow, I need to go to the store.

Queen gets up from the couch David Follows her.

                         DAVID
                       Baby wait-

                         QUEEN
          No David you wait! I'm not some little girl
          and we're not kids! We're damn near 40 years
                             old.

                         DAVID
                         Baby-

QUEEN
You know this is crazy, you need to handle your business. I'll be right back.

Queen turns to leave, David Grabs he by the arm she stiffens.

QUEEN
David.

He releases her arm.

QUEEN
Thank you. Now do what you gotta do, handle that. If you gotta go and meet her handle that, just let me know. Ok I'm leaving.

DAVID
Queen I love you.

QUEEN
In a minute David.

DISSOLVE TO:

INT. DELILAH'S LIVING ROOM - MORNING

Jason is sitting back enjoying himself pretending he's Delilah through text.

JASON
He believes her too, bitch ass nigga was probably fucking raw. I-need-to-see-you-asap-what's-your-new-address?

CUT TO:

INT. DAVID'S LIVING ROOM - MORNING

David sees the text he grabs his head and texts Queen.

>   DAVID TXT:MSG
>   She does want to see me.

>   QUEEN TXT:MSG
>   Ok, let me know when it's done.

>   DAVID TXT:MSG
>   Ok baby I love you.

Queen leaves David on read. David sends his address to Jason.

>   DAVID TXT:MSG
>   17752 E. Fox Ct.

                                    CUT TO:

INT. DELILAH'S LIVING ROOM - MORNING

When Jason receives the address he jumps out and smashes out his blunt.

>   JASON
>   C'mon nigga we out!

                                    CUT TO:

INT. BROTHER HASSANS OFFICE - MORNING

Brother Hassan is straightening up, Billy is helping.

>   BILLY
>   You heard from David today?

>   HASSAN

No I haven't, he was supposed to call me after prayer.

BILLY
I haven't heard from him either.

HASSAN
Everything ok?

BILLY
Oh yea, yea hell yea I'm good.

Billy scratches his head he is unsure.

FADE TO:

INT. DOCTORS OFFICE - MORNING

Delilah sits on a hospital bed alone, not looking herself then her Doctor walks in.

DOCTOR 2
Mrs. Johnson.

DELILAH
Yes.

DOCTOR 2
Congratulations! Test results came back positive, you're pregnant. Here are a few packets concerning your age I do have to advise you of the potential risks and complications through your pregnancy.

DELILAH
You know what you can save it. You don't know anything about what my black body is capable of, you probably put all types of little black girls on birth control without parents

permission so you can have "they" insides all fucked up, but I'm good honey, thank you.

Delilah is now on her feet and nearly dressed.

                    DOCTOR 2
        Well that was rather rude and uncalled for.

                    DELILAH
        Look thanks for the great news, if I could get
                a moment I'm trying to leave.

                    DOCTOR 2
            Have a good day Mrs. Johnson.

The Doctor leaves mad and embarrassed.

                    DELILAH
                Please be David's

                                        FADE TO:

INT. GROCERY STORE - MORNING

Queen is shopping, she passes by the pregnancy test pauses and thinks with curiosity, she then notices a bathroom not to far away, she then grabs the test and heads towards the bathroom.

                                        FADE TO:

INT. LAW ENFORCEMENT OFFICE - MORNING

A FBI Lieutenant is briefing officers for an assignment

                    LIEUTENANT

This is our target, he's a domestic terrorist and he has been forging documents to leverage real estate near east of Downtown Denver. We don't know exactly what he plans to do with his control but we must stop him before this goes any further. Do not under estimate this target if it wasn't necessary to remove the perp we wouldn't. I hand selected you two for this assignment, you're the best candidates we got. Nerves of still, and a history of carrying out orders precisely without question. Now here's the targets location…

DISSOLVE TO:

INT. DAVID'S LIVING ROOM – MORNING

David is laying on his couch looking distraught, he's been praying and meditating to no avail.

INTERCUT DAVID PRAYING, JASON IN ROUTE, AGENTS IN ROUTE

The Federal agents are 1st to get in position at David's house, then Jason Pulls up after, Jason texts David, Jason is still pretending he is Delilah.

JASON TXT MSG
I'm here

David sees the message and goes outside, watching David from a Birds eye view we also see power lines. The poem "Concrete Jungle" by Rico Garcia begins.

INTERCUT SEQUENCE

Visually we see flashbacks and foreshadowing ie: Queen and Delilah big pregnant hugging. The sequence ends with the last line of the poem.
David is approaching Delilah car with heavily tinted windows, as he approaches the Federal agents make their move. David looks up, Jason jumps out the car shooting, the agents fire shotgun shells into David's back in response to the gun blasts, Jason hits David in the head, Jason has a shoot out with agents.

FADE TO:

TODAY

INT. QUEEN'S KITCHEN - MIDDAY

Queen is lost a blank stare on her face dry tear marks down her cheek, the radio is on talking about last weeks events.

    RADIO PERSONALITY
I mean it was one thing back when the summer of violence took place they were shooting up there own neighborhoods, what took place last Saturday was a form of domestic terrorism.

    RADIO PERSONALITY 2
Exactly we have 3 gang banging thugs firing military grade weapons, killing two innocent bystanders and leaving us to clean up the mess.

    RADIO PERSONALITY
And one of these guys was posing as a community activist, imagine what his following is thinking, I mean-

Queen turns of the radio, she grabs he positive pregnancy test off the counter.

                              FADE OUT:

THE END

CONCRETE JUNGLE

A SPOKENWORD

BY RICO GARCIA

In the concrete jungle powerlines is vines,
And the tears of mothers of lost children that flood the streets is rivers.
Sinners.
Brothers and Siters.
Animals, carnivores and cannibals, and we feast on misery.
Misery is what we feast on, until we old and tired and our teeth gone.
And we play songs!
That to you sound ignorant, but it's a reason that everybody's feeling it, from Waverly to Aurelius
Really it's

A Symphony.
Or an Orchestra.
Orchestrated by the leaders behind it, you see there's healing in it if you ain't lived it you gotta find it.

In the concrete jungle powerlines is vines,
And each has its own story to tell.
It's own version of hell.
We have sex young here if you a virgin you frail.
And the shit just goes thru cycles, just watch it as I do.
Tupac used to be my idol.
Now I really just want a rifle,
Light up 16 candles wait for god to come
And ask him questions about this bible.

In the concrete jungle powerlines is vines,
And each makes 100's of connections.
And to them we all niggers,
No matter the complexion.
But we're blind to that,
And avoid the facts of how we truly act.
You see nigger is a word that describes ignorant,
Not a pigmentation.
And your smile is your own acknowledgement of your ignorance, do you hear what I'm saying?
Because ignorance is bliss,
And you guilty by affiliation,
One people one nation.

In the concrete jungle powerlines is vines,
That we Swing on,
Climb on,
Write on,

Rhyme on,
Get High on,
Til we Die on,
Diamonds!
In the rough.
Waiting to be found
We lost names
They still will settle for a slave deal
A whip and A chain
Or
Just 15 minutes of fame.
No one knows who to blame,
Tho most of us have noticed,
But we just cry or feel ashamed
Because they think it's the end of the world.
When it's just the dawning of the age.

In the concrete jungle powerlines is vines,
And buildings is like mountains.
Parking lots would then have to be valleys,
Cave and tombs a lot like these alleys,
But bricks ain't bricks.
Zips ain't on jackets.
Bowls ain't dishes.
And keys ain't on piano's.
You can get as high as you want!
That doesn't make you a soprano.
A house is not a home without some memorabilia
of Al Pacino
It's silly yes we know.
But don't blame us.
We just people.
Aren't you people?
Don't you breathe like we do?
And if you lucky won't that be the very thing
that
kills you?

In the concrete jungle powerlines is vines,
And often a father is still a son.
And sometimes it's the daughter who raises her mother.
You see why this is thought to be a place like no other?
All your issues can weigh a ton,
And your best friend could be a gun.
But although you're in this concrete jungle
Living the struggle
Ripping your muscles
I know you gotta hustle.
But I just want you to look up.
And know that the sun, I still the sun
                      son   son.

Made in the USA
Columbia, SC
30 March 2021